FALL

HARD

SUN CITY #2

JADE CHURCH

FALL HARD BY JADE CHURCH FIRST PUBLISHED IN GREAT
BRITAIN BY JADE CHURCH IN 2023

EBOOK ISBN: 978-1-7391457-2-9

PAPERBACK ISBN: 978-1-7391457-3-6

HARDBACK ISBN: 978-1-7391457-4-3

CONDITIONS OF SALE

CONTENT WARNING

Fall Hard contains themes and content that some readers may find triggering, this includes: *references to anxiety and depression, misogyny, homophobia, alcohol and drug use, sexual harassment, on-page sex, and swearing.*

ALSO BY JADE CHURCH

Temper the Flame

This Never Happened

Get Even (Sun City #1)

In Too Deep (Living in Cincy #1)

The Lingering Dark (Kingdom of Stars #1)

Three Kisses More

Coming Soon:

Tempt My Heart (Living in Cincy #2)

Strip Bare (Sun City #3)

The Clarity of Light (Kingdom of Stars #2)

Keep in touch!

Don't want to miss new release details, behind the scenes sneak peeks, cover reveals, sales, and more? Then sign up to my newsletter to get swoony romance updates straight to your inbox!

https://linktr.ee/jadechurchauthor

PLAYLIST

10:35 – Tiësto, Tate McRae
Flowers – Miley Cyrus
Dancing's done – Ava Max
Only Love Can Hurt Like This – Paloma Faith
golden hour – JVKE
Love Again – Dua Lipa
She's Thunderstorms – Arctic Monkeys
WANTED U – Joji
Glitch – Taylor Swift
Pretty Please – Dua Lipa

For everyone trying to find their own way

FALL
HARD

SUN CITY #2

JADE CHURCH

CHAPTER ONE

LOVE SUCKS. I WASN'T MUCH OF AN EXPERT, I'D only really fallen once—but there was only one thing worse than loving someone who didn't love you, and that was watching them fall in love with someone else. So there I was, about to do something that was probably a terrible idea—but lately all my ideas seemed terrible, so what could one more hurt?

I'd gotten to the club earlier than I cared to admit and immediately headed to the bar for a drink—I'd made a mistake not having anything before I came out, that was for sure. Luckily, the neon rainbow stripes that encased the front of the bar had made it easy to spot and I'd claimed a seat there on the tall black bar stools with ease.

I had been to a club only once in my life, when I'd just turned eighteen and managed to sneak out of the house, and I'd forgotten how loud and... sticky, they were. Dark too, only the rainbow lights tracing the edges of the walls, DJ booth, and the small smattering of tables tucked into a

1

few alcoves adding a soft multi-coloured glow to the room.

The girl I'd been watching for the past half-hour pushed away from the bar and made her way to a packed corner of the club. Her blonde hair was an unnatural white that seemed to change color with the disco lights and was almost the same color as her skin. I kept my eyes on her retreating figure as she paused by a skinny white guy wearing a ripped tee emblazoned with Britney Spears' face. Her hand dipped into the pocket of her high waisted jeans as she leaned in close to the guy, then she moved back to the bar. Done. Easy. I could do this. Probably.

I sighed, barely even feeling the buzz of the last three drinks I'd had against the strange tingling numbness that moved through my chest recently. It had been happening for a while, ever since I'd moved to Sun City and accidentally fallen in love with my best friend.

She was out with everyone else right now, gone to some football match her boyfriend, Ryan, was playing in and I'd told them I had to study. I snorted into my cocktail at the thought. I couldn't even remember the last time I'd gone to class.

I waited til she reclaimed her seat a little further down from mine and then I ordered another drink, the steady pulse of Christina Aguilera's *Dirty* making my heart feel like it thudded too hard. Her top was red and off the shoulders, not unlike something Jamie might have worn—

I gulped the drink the bartender handed me as I shook off the thought.

"Whoa. Steady there. You know they put alcohol in

those things, right?" The girl grinned at me and I swallowed before offering her a smile. If you didn't know better, then what I was about to ask her might seem perfectly natural coming from my lips—tonight, I looked the epitome of a party girl. I'd loosely curled my hair and let it run free over my shoulders, put on my highest pink velvet chunky heels and let my sparkly eye make-up be the only accessory needed to match the pink sequin mini dress.

"Well, there's a little mixer too. Got to stay hydrated." I laughed breathlessly and bit my lip as the girl's eyes moved over my bronze legs, made longer by my heels, and back up to my face. "Listen..." I leaned in close and a flirty smile tugged up the corners of her mouth. "I, um, was wondering if you have any pills?"

She leaned back, a look that might have been disappointment flashing across her face as a cheer went out in the crowd at the next song, before she nodded. "Sure. What are you looking for?"

"Ah, you know."

An eyebrow raised at my answer and I wanted to curse. "Sure, but do you?" I didn't answer and she rolled her eyes. "Look, are you sure you want to—"

"I'm sure," I said firmly. "I've just never done this before. My friend usually buys," I lied, clearing my throat a little and her eyes narrowed slightly before she nodded.

"Fine. How many do you want?"

"Just one."

Another eyebrow raise. Crap. I was so clearly out of my depth. I'd thought this would be good for me, to get out of my own head for a while, but maybe it was just another mistake.

"Thirty," the girl said and I barely held in my surprise. That seemed like a lot for one pill, but I couldn't say for sure if she was ripping me off or if I was just hopelessly naive. Either way, it didn't matter. Thirty dollars was nothing in the face of the inheritance my parents had given me to essentially stay out of their lives, another form of hush money—their signature move.

I slipped the cash out of my clutch and she rolled her eyes as I tried to be surreptitious about it and failed.

"Have a good night," she said dryly, handing me a clear baggie and then shoving away from the bar.

"You too," I murmured, the words lost in an old Taylor Swift song as I shook the pill free and examined it closely. Was I supposed to take the whole thing? I glanced around to see if I could maybe ask the white-haired drug dealer but she'd disappeared into the crowd on the dancefloor. I didn't even know what this thing was or how it would make me feel—what if I had an allergic reaction? I tried to shake the thought off. *What would Jamie do?*

Jamie would have already taken the pill by now and not given it a second thought. Yet here I was, having second, third, and fourth thoughts. I didn't need to do this—not to have a good time, and not to prove anything. But I just felt like I needed... *something*. Change, or maybe just an end to the aching hollowness that seemed to follow me around lately. It had been a rough year.

My palms were getting sweaty and I tossed the pill back and forth between my hands, not wanting it to melt or something. *Just do it.* I let out a slow breath as I brought my hand to my mouth and then paused. Was I supposed to swallow it whole? Chew it? Crap, I should have just asked Jamie—

I reined my thoughts in before I could get lost in my own head again, wondering what she was doing right now, whether the match had ended and they'd all gone to *The Box* for drinks after. *She's with Ryan. Her boyfriend. Having a great time without you.*

I swiveled the seat so I faced outwards and could watch the dancers, the ache in my chest reverberating around the bass of the music.

She was the reason I'd come here. Jamie. Or one of them, at least.

There were people like Jamie, so comfortable in their skin it seemed almost inhuman to me. She'd had her nudes leaked by her ex and was barely phased. She didn't break. How could you not envy someone like that? Who knows exactly who they are?

"For you," the green-haired bartender said from behind me and I looked up in surprise as a shot of tequila was placed next to me on the purple counter, alongside a cocktail.

"Oh, sorry! I didn't order this."

"No, doll. *She* did." He smiled at me and nodded his head off to the left where a familiar, blonde head smirked at me. Bryn.

"Right," I murmured, opting not to pick it up. "Thanks."

I hadn't exactly come here looking for company, not

the familiar kind anyway. I came here to get lost, to be someone new. While I knew from the way she flirted every time she saw me that Bryn would happily take me home and help me forget, I didn't look Bryn's way again.

For one night, I wanted to be someone else—someone unafraid to take risks, who doesn't pause to think or rationalize all the different ways a situation could go wrong, someone *scary*. That was one of the things I loved about Jamie. With her, you never knew what might happen next.

And so I found myself in a gay nightclub, buying drugs for the first time, getting ready to dance with strangers, just so I could pretend for a little while. To escape my own skin, like I wasn't the girl in love with her best friend, the girl that got kicked out of school, or the girl disowned by her parents. I put the pill on my tongue and swallowed it with the last of my drink before the shaking of my hands could persuade me to rethink my decision. Tonight, I was free.

How long would it take to kick in? I swung my legs idly to the beat and returned the smiles of a few people dancing in the middle of the floor. It wasn't a big club and the bar took up a lot of room, spanning the whole of the back wall, but the layout twisted and turned into small nooks where people were laughing or making out. Posters had lined the walls in the tiny corridor that had led to this larger dance floor, advertising the events coming up, so I knew that on Fridays they did karaoke and there was a drag show one Monday a month. Karaoke made me think of her though, not that what Jamie did with her voice should be cheapened down that way, and I fanned myself with my hand lightly as the heat from the club made my cheeks flush. Or maybe that was just the alcohol—it was wild to think about how far I'd come since leaving St Agatha's, the religious college I'd been kicked out of after being caught in a kiss with my female teacher. I had a fake ID, because I wasn't going to be twenty-one for another ten months, I was fully independent, and my dress just about covered my ass.

I sighed as I reached absently for the drink Bryn had sent over, dumping the tequila into the tall glass of orange liquid. This wasn't working. Sitting in a club and waxing poetic about my best friend was the exact opposite of what I was trying to do there.

The drink was fruity and sweet and I wrinkled my nose as I sipped it. I was pretty picky about the cocktails I drank, and this one was a little too syrupy to really be my thing, but the guy behind the bar was busy and I was thirsty. So overly sweet, flirty cocktail it would have to be.

The rhythm of the music changed to something bassier, the thud of it echoing through my chest as I let my shoulders relax. I glanced to my right and smiled at the pretty redhead collecting her drink. She had freckles similar to mine, coasting along her nose daintily, and her dress was a green silk that looked so weightless on her it could have floated away.

"Wanna dance?" I half-shouted over the music and then swallowed the rest of my drink quickly when she nodded with a big grin, grabbing my hand and tugging me out into the middle of the floor. Now, not everyone at gay clubs was actually gay, she could just be there with friends, but when she stepped closer and slipped a pale arm around my waist to tug me closer, I melted. She smelled like summer flowers, sweet and heady, and her gold eyeliner sparkled in the lights of the dance floor as her eyes dropped to my lips.

I didn't even know her name. But that was exactly what I'd wanted, right?

We laughed and swayed our hips to the music, a song I vaguely recognized but wasn't paying much attention to as the room swirled into a haze of rainbow lights and glitter.

"I love your eyeliner," I said into the redhead's ear, letting my lips brush the shell, and she grinned at me. "Pretty," I breathed as I pulled away and stroked a thumb idly underneath her eye.

The song changed, something heavy and angsty that made us throw our hands in the air and jump as high as we could manage without breaking an ankle in our towering heels. A group of people waved to her off to my right and she kissed my cheek before dancing over to them. I waved her off airily, not even feeling the disappointment as I swayed and bounced to the music, barely feeling the hands on my skin as I twirled between dancers. I don't know when I closed my eyes, couldn't remember deciding to do so, but the room felt like it was overwhelming my senses in a riot of color and sparkles when they flickered open. The cheesy disco lights were going strong and the girl I was dancing with had glitter in her hair that I stroked fondly, twining it around my finger as her brunette strands shone red under the lights.

This was what I'd been looking for, to just get lost for a little while. The emptiness in my chest that had threatened to overwhelm me the longer I stayed in the apartment had faded, replaced with laughter and the scent of honey shampoo.

Someone bought me a drink. Then two, then three, and the next set of hands that settled lightly on my waist steadied me when I hadn't even realized I'd been swaying.

They smelled nice, like jasmine or clementine, something flowery that danced on the edge of fruity. I inhaled deeply as I rested my head on their shoulder, slow dancing despite the Carly Rae Jepson song that blasted out around us.

I didn't want to move, tiredness settling into my arms and legs as I relaxed in this stranger's arms, but my throat was parched. I pulled away slightly too fast and bit the inside of my cheek as the pleasant haze I'd been drifting in threatened to send me down a swirling ravine that I knew would leave me puking.

"Sorry," I slurred. "Need another drink."

"I think what you need is to go home."

I wrinkled my nose. That voice sounded familiar.

I forced my eyes open and squinted in the flashing lights—when had they turned on a smoke machine? I clutched the woman's arm as I fought to assess myself for a second. It wasn't often that a smoke machine could trigger my asthma but for some reason my lungs felt sluggish anyway, like I was breathing in syrup.

"Hey, you're okay." The voice was so strong that my body relaxed, like it had just been waiting for orders. "Come on, I'll take you home."

A slither of coherency cracked through my senses and I frowned as I focused on familiar blue eyes that were, annoyingly, pinched with concern.

"I'm not going home with you."

Bryn rolled her eyes, thick dark lashes casting fascinating shadows across the high points of her cheeks and I struggled to focus on her words for a moment. "I'm not propositioning you, Olivia. You're absolutely fucked right now. You need to go home."

A giggle burst out of my mouth and I clamped a hand over my lips before letting it drop. "You said fuck."

Bryn wound an arm through mine and tried to guide me to the exit. "Come on."

"No."

We ground to a halt and a breath that even I could recognize as sheer exasperation escaped her.

"No?"

"No, I'm not going to sleep with you."

"Oh, sweetheart. I doubt you could even locate a boob right now—I'm taking you to *your* home, not mine."

Without thinking, I reached out and placed a hand on her chest. She was wearing a gauzy silver mesh top that sparkled prettily and I instantly coveted it, especially because it managed to feel silky rather than scratchy. We both looked down at the hand that cupped her left breast. It was full, bigger than my palm could comfortably cover, and Bryn looked bemused as she reached out and gently tugged my hand away.

"Come on."

I didn't argue. I would probably feel a thousand shades of embarrassed about this tomorrow, but right now I couldn't deny that the thought of my bed waiting for me sounded like bliss. Well, that and maybe some fries. Salty, greasy, goodness.

"Yes, yes, fine, we can stop for fries if somewhere is open."

I blinked, not realizing I'd said the last part aloud. Whatever. As long as I got my fries, I didn't care that I'd touched Bryn's boob. Plus, Sun City was a student town —of course someone would be selling fries at... I checked my phone and hissed as the brightness seared my eyes. Wow. Three AM. Not bad. Not bad at all.

I didn't think I'd gone out partying by myself in, well, ever and tonight I'd actually had a good time. There weren't many times in my life that I'd been able to just feel... good. Carefree.

"I'm sorry to hear that," Bryn said as she steered me around a bush that had appeared out of nowhere and I blinked at her in confusion.

"Am I still saying all this to you out loud? I thought I was just thinking stuff."

Bryn snorted. "Jesus you're wasted. What did you even take?"

"A pill."

"Of?"

I shrugged and the pinched look on Bryn's face

reappeared again but I tuned out before she could try and lecture me some more.

Fingers snapped in front of my face and I waved my hand in protest. "What?" I glanced around us, confused. "Where are we?"

Bryn's hand cupped my jaw, tilting my face up to look into her eyes and for the first time I realized she was slightly taller than me. I tugged my face free from her grip.

"You mean you don't remember the part of this very, *very* long walk home where you whined and complained until I agreed to go to *Paulies* with you to get fries?" She shook her head, somehow still managing to look good even under the gross fluorescent lights in the diner.

"I think these lights are giving me a hangover." I grimaced as I tried to shield my eyes with my hand but a second later the pain was forgotten as a carton of hot fries was pressed into my palm. "You are beautiful," I moaned, shoveling two in my mouth and wincing slightly at the burn. There was only one thing ruining this.

I thrust the fries into Bryn's arms and she fumbled slightly as she caught them.

"What are you—"

I reached down and unclasped my shoes, sighing in relief as my toes touched the cold tiled floor.

"Liv, no—"

I grabbed my fries back out of Bryn's hands and spun for the door, the world whirling around me as I moved too quickly.

The night air was cool and still smelled like heat from earlier in the day. It was late—or early, depending on how you looked at it—but plenty of people still milled around. Bryn caught up to me a second later, my shoes dangling from their straps in her hands as she muttered under her breath.

"Your feet are going to get cold."

"They're fine," I said absently, munching on a fry as I started away from the town and down the path that led through the park. Despite it being paved, the twigs and errant rocks immediately stabbed into the soles of my feet and I hopped a little as I walked, trying not to drop my food. "Ow."

The trees were bushy and full, though it was too dark to see the lush green they'd turned a little while back, and the moon just peaked out from between branches. For a second I just stood there, staring up at the sky as I continued to eat my fries, the stars swirling around my head and the night air barely touching my skin. My hand scraped the bottom of the box and I frowned as I stared down into it.

A sigh startled me and I turned wobbily to see Bryn watching me. "You want to stare at the stars some more or can we get you home? You must be cold."

"It's the summer."

"It's also almost four in the morning."

"Huh."

I hobbled forward a few more steps and Bryn watched me, shadows partially obscuring whatever expression was on her face—not that I particularly cared what she thought anyway.

"Come on." She turned so her back was to me and I

waited for her to walk away, confused when she crouched a little. "Well? Are you coming?"

I stepped carefully across the small distance separating us and hopped onto her back, her arms coming up under my legs as I hooked mine around her neck.

"Do *not* throw up on me."

I giggled as we walked, a little confused about what we were doing and how we'd got there—didn't Bryn live up by the mall? *So why was she walking with me through the park?* The odd swaying motion soothed me until my cheek was pressed against her hair and I jumped when she nudged me before sliding me off her back. I stumbled and her arms caught me under my elbows, our faces close enough in the dark that we could have kissed.

Her eyes were so blue that they stood out against the darkness, and I stepped closer as my eyes dropped to her mouth. I'd noticed that Bryn was beautiful before, you would have to be blind not to, but she seemed practically luminescent in the dark.

"Liv—"

My mouth brushed across hers, featherlight, reminding me of another kiss, another girl as I fought the haze descending on me, sighing as our mouths parted. "Jamie..."

Bryn slid away and I hadn't realized how cold I was until her warmth left. She fumbled around in the dark, reaching under the matt for the spare key Jamie and I left there and unlocking the door.

"Come on," she said quietly, guiding me inside and

helping me into bed when I pointed to my room across the hall.

I shimmied my dress up and over my head and heard Bryn leave as I climbed into bed naked, not bothering to wash off my make-up.

"Here," she said a second later, setting a glass of water down on my immaculately tidy bedside table and then straightening again to leave.

I caught her hand before she could go. "Stay."

"Liv, I really don't—"

"Please," I mumbled as I snuggled down into my comforter and lifted the edge for her to join me. I relaxed once she slid off her shoes and settled next to me. "Stay."

"Go to sleep, Olivia."

"Bryn?"

"What?"

"I'm sorry I touched your boob."

She chuckled quietly and the sound followed me into a dreamless sleep.

CHAPTER TWO

THE WHOLE *DON'T DO DRUGS* SPIEL SUDDENLY made a lot more sense in light of the hangover from hell that I currently had. My body had naturally woken up around seven in the morning and I'd laid in bed in quiet agony as my head throbbed. Bryn had been curled up facing away from me and my arm had gone numb under her head. I'd made the executive decision right then that I was still not sober enough to deal with everything I could vaguely remember doing last night, or the very warm Bryn still in my bed. So I'd gone back to sleep and only woke up again when my bladder demanded that I get out of my covers.

By the time I made it out of the bathroom, figuring I might as well shower seeing as I was in there and the bottoms of my feet were filthy, Bryn had left and Jamie had only just got home. I'd somehow made it through the afternoon without puking and by the time we got to *The Box* in the evening I was regretting my decision to sign up for the new yoga class up by the mall. At least Bryn had opted not to come to the bar, that way I didn't have to deal with my own shame as well as the usual jealousy that took root inside me whenever I spent time with Jamie and Ryan. They'd left fairly quickly after dropping the bomb that Jamie wasn't going to be expelled and she had signed a preliminary record deal. All in the same day. If I didn't love her so much, I might have hated her.

I'd snuck out of the bar not long after they did, hesitating between heading back to the apartment and running the risk of finding them there too, or going to yoga class like I'd ambitiously planned prior to experiencing the worst hangover of my life.

And yet, I would have rather thrown up doing the downward dog than potentially listened to Jamie and Ryan having sex next door. Of course, as soon as I actually arrived at the class I regretted that decision.

I stopped short in the doorway to the studio at the sight of a long pair of legs stretching idly. Crap.

I walked in slowly, knowing I couldn't walk away now without looking conspicuous, and set my bag down near the edge of the room. I'd changed into some stretchy yoga pants and a sports bra in the restroom on my way in, knowing I couldn't do anything in my jeans, but now felt slightly vulnerable as people continued to file in and the cool air brushed my bare arms.

Bryn hadn't noticed me yet, or maybe she had and was just pretending not to see me after our encounter last night. I tried not to cringe as I remembered all the dumb stuff I'd said and done—but not all the memories were unpleasant. I'd had a good time, mostly. And for a while when I'd been dancing with Bryn, oblivious to who I'd had my arms around, it had felt like the most comfortable place in the world. I was never going to live it down.

Bryn looked up at that moment and our eyes met, her blue eyes going wide and her arms freezing mid-air as they reached up to fix her perky blonde ponytail.

Great. Now it looked like I'd been staring at her— which, yeah, I guess I kind of had been but not like *that*.

She took a step forward, like she was going to come over and talk to me, and I quickly spun away, pretending to rummage in my bag on the floor for something and then busying myself with a sip from my water bottle.

"Amazing to see so many new faces tonight!" the instructor called at the front of the room, her smile so wide I felt like I could see every single one of her teeth. "We'll start with a few warm-up stretches and then I'm going to put you in pairs just for the final stretching exercise, okay?"

A chorus of *Okays!* sounded back at her and I jumped. Was this yoga or a pep rally?

She talked us through a series of stretches, nodding and smiling encouragingly as she walked between us, correcting form as necessary. Once she got back to the front of the room I felt like I breathed a little easier, having not enjoyed her walking around behind me.

She clapped her slightly orange hands together and closed her eyes. "Now let's take a moment to breathe before we complete the final stretch."

I shook my arms out before letting them hang loosely

at my side, no longer feeling the chill of the room after the first ten minutes of the class. It had been a while since I'd done any yoga or pilates and my muscles were shaking a little already. We breathed out for five and in for five before the instructor opened her eyes and offered us all a smile.

"Right, get into your usual pairs then please girls and I'll have my two new ladies together here at the front too."

My heart felt like it stopped in my chest. She was talking about me. Me and...

Bryn.

Because, of course. Why would the universe give me a break for a single freaking second?

I walked over reluctantly and avoided looking at Bryn, instead focusing all my attention on the instructor as she talked us through the next movement and I felt myself pale. I looked to Bryn and she raised an eyebrow coolly at me.

"You want to go first? Or shall I?"

I held in a sigh and laid down on her yoga mat, keeping my hips squared as I lifted my legs and let her catch them. This was going to be awkward.

Her hands were warm on my calves and when she leaned forward I could see down her sports bra to the full chest I'd touched last night in the club. I looked away hastily, breathing out when she told me to as she pressed my legs towards my chest.

"Don't forget to breathe, darling," the instructor said as she paused next to us. There wasn't a drop of sweat on her skin, so it was definitely only me that had felt the strain thus far.

I breathed out as Bryn pushed forwards again, stretching me, and gave the instructor a strained smile before she walked away, her long brown braid thumping cheerfully at the center of her back.

Bryn looked at me from the other side of my legs and our stare caught and held as her hands slid to hold my knees.

"Very good, now pull back and let's form our V-shape before we try again."

I could feel my cheeks heating as I parted my legs and Bryn watched me in silence, though her eyes seemed to darken as she stepped between them and pushed down until my feet were nearly by my head.

"Very flexible," the instructor chirped as she walked up and down.

"Very," Bryn murmured and I knew I had to look like a tomato as she finally put my legs down and we swapped positions.

If it had been awkward before, then it was nothing compared to how I felt now being the one standing over her—feeling the strength in her legs as I pressed into her and she pushed into me, creating a resistance that would hopefully stretch the muscles perfectly.

She stopped pushing when the instructor called for us to swap into the high-V position, and I nearly slumped forward into her at the absence of the weight pushing against me.

God, I was never going to a yoga class again.

Jamie thinks I slept with Bryn. *Jamie thinks I slept with Bryn*. It was the only thought I could seem to form. It shouldn't have mattered, Jamie was with Ryan, she was happy and we were nothing more than friends. That was all we would ever be, and I knew that. I *accepted* that. Yet, I'd still let her think something more had happened between Bryn and I than actually had. Or rather, I hadn't worked that hard to correct the assumption when she'd made it after seeing Bryn leave here the other night anyway.

I wasn't trying to make her jealous, exactly... because why would she care? She'd been practically purring when she'd thought Bryn had 'seduced' me. Of course, the truth was much more embarrassing—I'd kissed Bryn while I was wasted and called her someone else's name. And I'd touched her boob. *Then* probably made her think I was a stalker by turning up to the same yoga class as her and touching her legs a bunch.

I scrubbed a little harder at the dishes Jamie had left in the sink. If I never saw Bryn again, it would still be too soon. But considering her brother was friends with Jamie's boyfriend... I sighed as suds splashed up and soaked the front of my sweatshirt. I would just have to take a page out of Jamie's book and own it. So what if I'd kissed Bryn? So what if I'd drunkenly begged her to stay the night with me like a kid afraid of the dark?

I cringed. The second hand embarrassment was getting me even now, almost forty-eight hours later. I was actually still a bit hungover which didn't help and my feet ached something fierce just from the short walk Bryn had permitted while I'd been barefoot before she'd taken pity and carried me.

Considering we didn't know each other that well, I should probably be thanking her. Would flowers be okay? Or would that seem too romance-y? Like, *hey, sorry I touched your boob and you felt obligated to help me home from the club, hope you like freesias!* Okay, so not flowers then. Wine? No, no, that was a bit too... adult. Serious.

Crap. I was starting to feel nauseous from thinking about this too hard. Maybe it was just better if I didn't say anything and we could both just pretend that nothing had happened? It wasn't like I had to see Bryn *that* often, and when I did it was usually in a group setting.

I dried my hands on the towel and set about cleaning the counters and drying the dishes... so now I was stress cleaning. *Great.*

It had been fun letting loose the other night, but losing control wasn't everything it was made out to be. Especially not when it left you stress cleaning in your kitchen and trying to come up with a better plan than *ignore the problem and hope it goes away.*

I slowly set down the disinfectant spray and looked blankly at the spotless kitchen in front of me, the wooden countertops gleaming. I didn't need to think about any of this right now. I could just go back to bed, save this problem for another day.

A knock at the door made me mumble a curse under my breath as I grabbed the kitchen towel and dabbed a little frantically at my still-soaked front. I'd made sure the key under the matt had been replaced, so why would Jamie be knocking?

My mouth went dry as I walked up to the door and hesitantly cracked it open. Crap. We desperately needed to get a peephole.

"Hi," Bryn said, somewhat cautiously. It was the first time I'd seen her since yoga and I'd left before she could try and speak to me afterwards. She was probably wondering how much of the other night I could remember, and right then I wished it was a lot less.

"Are you stalking me?" I blurted and she blinked, one eyebrow rising up as she folded her arms across her chest. *Do NOT look at her chest!* I kept my eyes trained firmly on her face as she watched me silently but I wanted to scream because all I could think about was *itouchedherboob.* It was dumb. I wasn't some sixteen-year-old with a crush. I didn't even *like* Bryn. I mean, I didn't *dislike* her, but I didn't want to touch her boobs either—or anywhere else.

"Are you okay?" She peered at me, leaning in closer and I backed up reflexively. "Your face has gone all red."

"I'm fine," I rasped, mouth suddenly dry. "What are you doing here?"

A slight scuff in the hallway had me peering over her shoulder as Jamie, Kit, and Ryan appeared carrying a couple boxes and a suitcase.

No. Surely not.

"What's going on here?" I could hear the panic in my

own voice and Bryn frowned like she might try and comfort me. I retreated into the apartment as they all filed in and Jamie smiled at me, her dark eyes warm but clear.

"Bryn needs a place to crash for a few days. Her place flooded and I said it would be fine for her to stay on the sofa here. That's okay, right?"

I stared at her. It was her apartment, so really whatever Jamie wanted to do was her choice, but I still squinted at her dubiously for a second. Was this some kind of forced meet-cute?

"Are you high?"

Kit snorted and Jamie swatted at me. "Don't be rude, Liv. I've barely had a one-pop today."

I wasn't entirely sure what that meant, but she looked sober enough so I just shrugged and shoved down my panic. "Sure. Why not? It'll be... fun."

Ryan walked back into the hall, sans Bryn's suitcase, and Kit dropped a box onto the cheap wood floor at his own feet as he eyed the red hallway walls, running a hand through his blue hair. "*So* much fun." Kit smirked at me, his lip piercing flashing in the light, and I wanted to spontaneously perish on the spot. He knew. Of course he knew! Kit was Bryn's brother, so why wouldn't she tell him every excruciating detail of what had happened the other night?

"Well, I'd show you around but I know you're already familiar with the layout." Jamie waggled her dark brows at me behind Bryn's back and I shook my head at her before looking away as Ryan pressed a kiss to her cheek.

The thing was, he was a good guy. So I couldn't even

hate the fact that she loved him otherwise *I* would be the asshole. I opted to walk away and felt more than saw Bryn following.

"No room at your brother's place?" I asked nonchalantly and Kit glanced over at the sound of his name, strolling into the living room he'd helped us repaint a light pink not that long ago.

"I thought Bryn would be more comfortable in your bed—I mean, sofa." He grinned and I shot Bryn a pointed look that she ignored.

"Oh!" Jamie blinked around at the room as she walked in. "You cleaned. Like. Everywhere. Is, um, everything okay?"

"Why wouldn't it be?" I said probably a shade too fast and refused to allow myself to even blink in Bryn's direction again. "How long do you think you'll be staying?" I said directionlessly as I tugged at a loose thread on my sleeve. *Please just be a few nights. Please, please, please—*

"Just a few weeks I think." So close. "The flood was pretty bad. Apparently there was a leak that had been building for a long time and a lot of my stuff got wrecked when part of the ceiling finally collapsed."

Oh. Crap. Now I felt bad that I'd been more worried about her being here than showing any empathy or concern for the fact her home had been ruined. "Wow. What did you manage to salvage?"

"Luckily I had my laptop on me because I was in class when it happened, but a ton of my books are just mush and I'm going to be paying a fortune in drycleaning bills."

"That's fucked up." Jamie frowned in the way that meant she was probably considering something rash, the deep purple lipstick she was wearing made her eyes seem darker than usual and added an air of unpredictability to her that made the hair on my arms rise. "There's no way you're paying for any of that shit. If it was a college building, it's their responsibility. Right?" She looked between us all and Bryn smiled, a dimple popping in her cheek.

It was likely doubly amusing for her, considering she studied law. So she probably knew better than anyone what exactly the college was liable for, but I could tell she was pleased Jamie cared enough to fight for her. That was just Jamie though—the first time we met she'd kissed me to convince some creeper hitting on me at the bar that we were there together. Tongue first, names second. I think I'd fallen for her almost right then and there.

"I rent privately, but depending on what caused the flood the landlord should hopefully be paying for the damage."

"And emotional distress," Jamie said, nodding as she folded her arms across her chest, her black leather jacket wrinkling slightly at the motion.

Kit snorted as he ran a hand through his baby blue, semi-long hair. "Oh yeah, I think Bryn is going to be feeling *so* distressed that she has to stay here with Liv. Boo-hoo—"

Bryn smacked her brother's arm and I quirked an eyebrow at him. He was being unusually snarky towards me. Normally Kit and I got on well, but maybe... Was he being protective?

Jamie's dark eyes flashed as she turned and whispered something to Ryan that made him chuckle as he draped an arm around her waist before she looked back to Kit. "You are so cute, blue. Are you trying to defend your sister's honor? Because I'm pretty sure that ship sailed—"

I don't know what came over me but my mouth was opening and before I could think anything through I blurted, "I didn't sleep with Bryn!" Several pairs of eyes landed on me, so heavy their weight felt practically tangible. Jamie's mouth shut with a little click and her dark hair swayed slightly at her sharp jolt, brushing her chin. She'd cut it again recently and the blunt cut made her look even fiercer than usual. "Well, I mean, we did *sleep* together, but we didn't *sleep* together—"

"Okay..." Jamie laughed and it felt awkward in the quietness of the room. "Well, there's still time right?"

I rolled my eyes and Bryn flushed slightly.

"Hey, we were just going to drop Bryn's stuff off here and then head to *The Box*. Do you want to come?" Ryan smiled, his dimples popping as he peered at me from where his head rested on the top of Jamie's and I forced a smile out from behind clenched teeth back at him.

"Sure. Is Kat coming?"

"Technically," Jamie laughed a little and I could have bottled the happy sound and drank it, even if the reason for that happiness was tall, dark-haired and vaguely resembled *Superman*.

"She's working?" I confirmed, feeling a little bad that

we were all going to rock up to the bar and make Kat watch us laugh and have fun without her. She and Jamie had a love-hate relationship, they fought like sisters but I knew they would kill for each other—not that it took much to move Jamie to violence.

"Her shift finishes soon, so I said we'd meet her there for a drink."

"Okay, well, you guys go on ahead. I'm going to get changed and then I'll walk over." One of the best things about Jamie's apartment was that it was right in the center of town, so most things weren't too far to walk to—though Radclyffe's college campus was probably furthest but of course getting to class on time wasn't as high a priority for Jamie as easy access to iced coffee from *Cocoa & Rum.* Admittedly, going to class had been pretty low on my priority list recently too, I just couldn't bring myself to be motivated enough to care about it. I mean, it was *communications,* hardly rocket science, so when I was in class my mind wandered anyway. Usually straight to Jamie.

They headed back out into the hall and Bryn lingered in the doorway before she left, a question in her eyes that had a lump rising in my throat. It was clear what she was asking—*Was I really okay with this?* I gave her a quick nod before hurrying into my room.

Regardless of how awkward it might be to have her here, she needed somewhere to stay and I wasn't a complete asshole. Besides, she would have class and I would have... stuff, so we probably wouldn't be home at the same time that much anyway.

I shucked off my sweatshirt as soon as I got into my room and draped it over the handle of my wardrobe to dry before I put it in the hamper. At least Kat would be at *The Box*. I just had to survive the time it took for her to shift to end on the bar and come and sit down with us. I traded my leggings for jeans and grabbed a green tee and denim jacket before heading out. I was beyond happy that it was starting to get hot again, the days long and the evenings so warm that my jacket would be enough for the walk to and from the bar.

The Box wasn't far from the apartment, but the few minutes walk helped clear my head a little so I could mentally prepare to hang out with people. I was definitely the introvert to Jamie's extrovert, my social battery tended to drain pretty quickly at which point I needed to retreat to somewhere quiet with a book or movie.

Thankfully, it wasn't open mic night today and the bar was semi-quiet, most people probably off cramming for end of semester exams. I should have been doing the same, but I couldn't bring myself to stress out about a degree I didn't even want to complete. It was still relatively early in the day, so the lights in the bar were a light pink that would deepen to red as the evening went on and the small stage opposite the bar was empty.

I spotted Jamie and the others in our usual booth toward the back of the bar on the left and gave them a quick wave before heading to the middle for a drink. Kat wasn't there, so I could only hope that meant she was done with her shift and was out in the kitchen or something. The bartender who served me would have been cute if I'd swung that way, but I smiled at him regardless and thanked him for the rum and coke he slid my way after flashing him my fake ID. It wasn't long now until I wouldn't need it, though my parents had opted to give me my inheritance at eighteen, so drinking was about the only perk I'd be receiving when my birthday rolled around.

I turned to head to the booth and nearly bumped into a redhead who looked vaguely familiar. She blew me a kiss and I smiled weakly when I realized she was the girl from the club who'd had on the golden eyeliner. That got me thinking about how badly I needed to add a gold to my repertoire, it had looked stunning on her.

"Who was that?" Jamie asked as soon as I sat down.

I took a gulp of my drink to avoid answering. I wasn't sure why exactly I was hiding that I'd gone out the other night. Jamie had spontaneously driven to Phoenix to talk to a record producer and so she had no clue that I'd tried to let loose. I got the feeling that if I mentioned the pill I'd taken, she would disapprove. That would be a little hypocritical, of course, but I knew it would be coming from a place of concern.

"Oh, just someone I met a few nights ago."

Her mouth opened, probably to grill me for more details and I tried to hide my grimace and then relief when Ryan distracted her. She was doing an excellent Kat impression, that was for sure. Normally my other friend was the one digging down to get all the juicy details. I knew it was a quality Jamie only tolerated, but I found it to be both endearing and sad. It made me wonder what had happened in Kat's life that made her feel like she had to know absolutely everything as soon as she could. Either way, I didn't really want to get into any of what had happened the other night with Jamie. Not now, at least.

She turned back toward me and a flash of sympathy crossed Ryan's face as he glanced at me from beside her—he'd distracted her on purpose, clearly sensing my discomfort. Ugh. Such a nice guy. I cut Jamie off before she could even think to ask me anything else.

"So, Kit! How's football going?" I said brightly and faltered when he leveled blue eyes the same shade as his sister's on me as he slipped his phone back into his pocket.

"Season's over. It's nearly the summer."

He spoke so flatly that my stomach dropped, a familiar anxiety clawing its way inside as I tried to work out if I was just being overly sensitive or if he'd definitely sounded mad at me. Was this still about Bryn?

"What's crawled up your ass?" Jamie glared at him and I felt my shoulders relax. Okay, so it hadn't just been me who'd noticed Kit's weird behavior.

Kit said nothing, simply stood up from his spot on the end of the bench opposite me and walked out, leaving us staring after him in shock.

Bryn sighed. "Don't mind him, there's some stuff going on with him and Leo but he won't tell me what it is. It's had him in a foul mood for days though."

I was fairly confident that Kit was in love with Leo, and vice versa. Especially because Kat had once tried to flirt with him and Leo had been both completely oblivious and entirely disinterested. If it hadn't upset Kat so much, it would have been funny.

If I hadn't been desperate for Kat to turn up before, I was more so now. Bryn was looking at me strangely, like she was trying to decide whether or not to bring up some likely embarrassing memory from the other night, so I downed my drink and stood quickly, pressing my hands together in front of my body.

"I'm, ah, going to see what's keeping Kat and get another drink." I laughed nervously, practically a squeak, and then spun around in the direction of the bar. I waited there patiently for a few moments before noticing Bryn moving towards me in my periphery. Crap. There were too many people in front of me waiting to get served. I would have to escape another way.

I stood on my toes for a moment, searching for the sign for the restroom to see how long the queue was and breathed a sigh of relief that there was nobody there waiting. Without much of a crowd, Bryn could probably spot where I was headed but if I was quick enough maybe I could get in a stall and stand on the seat so she couldn't find me?

The ridiculousness of the thought made me pause before I decided, *fuck it,* and set off for the restroom at a pace even Bryn's long legs would struggle to match. Or so I thought.

A hand caught my elbow just as I stepped into the shadowy nook that precluded the ladies—so close, yet so far. Bryn gently tugged to turn me around and our chests rested against one another, mine moving at a much more rapid pace than hers as my breaths came fast.

"Olivia—"

I kissed her. Why? I had no idea. Her lips were soft, a detail I'd forgotten the other night, and her delicate perfume smelled pleasant as it filled the air around us.

She pulled back, blinking rapidly and looking more than a bit shocked. "What the hell did you do that for?"

"I don't know?" I practically shoved away from her as I tugged harshly on my ponytail. "I panicked! It just seemed like the right thing to do?"

Bryn snorted, her dimple flashing out at me and I scowled at it. "Well, I was trying to talk to you and make sure you were okay because I thought you were being weird back there, but that's nothing to how weird you were just then."

"I'm sorry," I groaned. "Everything's just felt so messy since the other night and I haven't known whether I should thank you or apologize or pretend that nothing happened at all." Bryn raised an eyebrow and I tried to read the expression on her face and failed. "Um, sorry? Thank you? I—"

I kissed her again and reared back when the door to the restroom flew open and Kat's wide green eyes met mine.

"You need to stop doing that," Bryn said dryly and I threw my hands up in the air.

"I'm sorry, I panicked!"

Kat looked between us, a hint of a smile playing

around her full lips as she tucked her curly brown hair behind her ear. "When did this happen?"

I shook my head frantically. "No. It's not. This," I gestured between myself and Bryn and then looked at my hand in horror when it touched her boob. "You know what, I'm just going to go."

"Wait, Liv." Bryn took my arm again and I blinked away the tears beginning to wet my eyes. What was wrong with me? Was this some kind of two-day come down? Was I still drunk? Or high? I'd kissed Bryn *twice* and Kat had seen. There was no way she would be able to keep this secret, she already looked fit to burst with questions. "It's okay. Just, I don't know, breathe. It's not a big deal. What's a kiss between friends, right?" Bryn grabbed Kat and kissed her full on the mouth, leaving her wide-eyed a second later when Bryn pulled back. "See? Not weird at all, right, Kat?"

"Um, yeah," Kat said, cheeks slightly pink. "Your lips are really soft."

"They totally are," I agreed. Bryn started laughing and I couldn't help but join in, some of that odd tension finally flowing away. "I'm sorry. I'm okay."

Bryn nodded. "Good." Kat looked a little confused but nodded along with us and Bryn shot me a puzzled look as I turned away from the ladies room. "Don't you need to go in there?"

"What? Oh. No."

"Then why—"

"I was going to climb onto one of the toilet seats to hide from you." Kat and Bryn stared at me and, admittedly, it sounded ten-times worse when I said it aloud. "Next round's on me?"

"Damn right." Bryn grinned and I couldn't help but smile back. Somehow, it felt like things might finally be okay.

CHAPTER THREE

Everything was not okay.

"Frankly, we're concerned. Your attendance is far below the expected percentage, you've failed to submit several assignments, and you are at serious risk of failing the course."

I should have been panicked, hearing those words. I could see the genuine worry on her face, her watery eyes squinting through her glasses as she studied me. Winters was easily one of the nicest professors I'd ever had. But I just didn't care.

Not so long ago, Jamie and Kat had told me that if I really wasn't enjoying studying on my course then I should quit. Drop out. It hadn't even occurred to me that dropping out was an option—for so long, I'd done whatever my parents wanted, and they'd wanted me to get a degree. So I'd gone to St Agatha's, been kicked out, and wound up studying Communications at Radclyffe purely because it was where they had room for me and I had no idea what I wanted to study. Of course, it occurred to me now that maybe I just didn't *want* to study at all.

"Okay," I said, crossing my legs primly. I had been dreading this meeting for days, hadn't told anyone just to avoid thinking about it. Jamie would have peppered me with questions or offered to beat someone up, Kat would have fussed and worried more than me and... Well, that was it really. I liked the rest of our circle of friends, but I wasn't as close with them one-on-one. So I had quietly let this anxiousness bubble away inside of me until the day of the meeting came and I realized I'd been anxious for nothing.

"Okay? Olivia, I don't think you understand the severity of the issue."

I nodded thoughtfully, barely paying her any attention as I let my eyes rove over the rest of her office space. Some professors kept things sparse, not Winters though. Every surface was covered with an assortment of crystals and fabrics, it felt more like the office of a psychic than a business and comms professor.

"I promise that I do, I'm just not sure that Communications is a great fit for me." I somehow got the words past my lips and felt an instant rush of lightheadedness at daring to voice the thought I'd been mulling over. I swallowed and felt my shoulders relax slightly when Winters nodded, tucking a piece of gray curly hair behind her ear as she leaned back in her chair.

"Ah, well maybe we can help with that." I raised my eyebrows, intrigued, and she continued with a gentle smile. "I understand your circumstances were... less than ideal, when you joined us, and while I can't guarantee you a place on a course in a different department, I can certainly facilitate a few taster sessions within your current one."

"So, like a business course?" I couldn't say I was that interested in business either. I'd done a short course as one of my electives at St Agatha's and it had nearly bored me to tears.

"Sure," Winters said easily, "or journalism, something in that vein. I can make enquiries with other departments if you'd like, but there's no guarantees."

Well, I didn't want her to waste too much of her time when I had no clue what I might be interested in. Maybe Kat and Jamie were right and academia just wasn't for me.

"Either way, we need to see immediate improvement in your commitment to your education. Otherwise, we will have no choice but to remove you from the course."

"I understand," I said finally, standing up and reaching forward to shake her hand. "A couple of taster sessions couldn't hurt." I was grateful, truly. It was nice that she was reaching out and that Radclyffe was making an effort, especially considering the treatment Jamie had experienced recently when her professor tried to have her expelled.

Of course, I knew a little something about expulsions myself. Though, mine had been a little more hush-hush than Jamie's. St Agatha's hadn't wanted the scandal of a student-teacher relationship (and a same-sex one at that) to 'tarnish' their reputation. My parents had been quick to agree.

I strode out of Winters' office after she'd promised to arrange things for me, musing silently as I walked, my thoughts now firmly elsewhere.

I was pretty sure the last time I'd spoken to my parents was when I'd moved out of St Agatha's and into Radclyffe's temporary student housing. They'd helped me move, but the silence had been icy and the tension, biting. I'd been glad when they'd gone.

Campus was relatively quiet. It was the inbetween-y time of not quite early but not quite afternoon and so the majority of students not in class were probably still sleeping off their late-night study sessions. It made me wonder what I'd have been doing right then if I had still been at St Agatha's. It was almost eleven-thirty, so I would probably have been in prayer. The thing was, I didn't think I'd always been disinterested in college. I'd liked being at St Agatha's, even if some of the girls were a little bitchy. It had changed something though, taken the shine away from learning, maybe, when they tossed me aside and my parents had followed suit.

The sky was so blue and with the misplaced anxiety surrounding that meeting now gone, I felt like I could properly enjoy it. I sent a quick mental thanks out into the world, glad that I was free to live the life I'd always wanted. Not that I was really sure what that life would look like, but it was *mine* to choose, to decide, and that's what I'd really craved this whole time.

I didn't have faith in the same way as my parents, in the way St Agatha's had wanted, but I still hoped, still believed there had to be something more. If there was a

God, I knew they'd listen regardless of whether I was in a church and that they'd accept me regardless of who I loved.

A hand touched my arm and I jumped, a shriek ripping free from my throat.

"Shit, sorry!"

I let out a breath of relief as I recognised the voice, and then the face, as I turned around. "Xander! Don't *do* that!"

"I'm sorry, I called your name but you didn't hear me." His brown eyes were wide and pinched at the corners and I took a deep breath in an effort to slow my pounding pulse.

"It's okay, I'm sorry. I was kind of lost in thought."

"Is everything alright?" He fell into step beside me and I half-smiled. It was always such a novelty to walk next to Xander, he was so tall that even I had to look up at him when he talked. Bits of his dark hair had escaped the bun he'd pulled it into, barely brushing the tops of his cheek bones.

It was a shame, really, that he did absolutely nothing for me. He was objectively beautiful and I knew he liked me, but I'd kissed a boy for the first time when I was twelve and hadn't been bothered about doing so again.

"Kind of. They might kick me off my course."

"What?" A startled dog yapped excitedly at Xander's near-shout and I swatted him on the arm half-heartedly as I cooed at the pup. "Didn't we just sort this exact thing out for Jamie?"

I shrugged. "The difference is that Jamie actually cared about her course."

"And you don't?"

"No," I said after a pause. "I really, really don't." We were quiet for a few minutes as we walked and I could feel his eyes on my face until I sighed and stopped moving. "What's wrong?"

"Nothing."

"Xander..."

"It's just, I don't know. You seem sad."

That was one of the things I liked about Xander, it wasn't often that he minced his words or refused to say what he was really thinking. I avoided him more than I should, purely because of his crush on me, but he knew I liked girls and had never had an issue with it. I guess we couldn't help who we loved.

"I'll be okay." I smiled a little and he studied my face before nodding firmly and we carried on. "What's new with you?"

He shrugged. "I feel like this is the first time I've left the house in ages, every time I blink I see textbook pages."

We laughed and fell into an easy rhythm as we got to the end of the park pathway, then he headed to *Cocoa & Rum* and I turned towards the apartment half-dreading finding Jamie there, and yet also half-hoping to see her face. She spent a lot of her time at Ryan's lately. I got the impression she thought I wasn't okay with him coming to our place, so I really never knew when she would be there. Though, I supposed that with the addition of Bryn to the space it wouldn't be as quiet when Jamie was gone. I couldn't decide whether that was an appealing thought or not.

We didn't really have much in the way of neighbors, just a couple of people semi-adjacent to our apartment, and I always thought it was funny that there was this idea of college being a place where you made friends, met people, fell in love. It was true that I'd done all of those things, and yet it was still one of the loneliest experiences of my life—that much hadn't changed between transferring from St Agatha's to Radclyffe.

I pushed open the door to the apartment and froze as the sound of loud Lo-Fi practically slapped me in the face. Jamie only listened to Lo-Fi when she was smoking, and I couldn't smell the tell-tale tang of weed, so I had to assume it was Bryn with the volume cranked right up in the living room. Strange, I'd had her pegged for more of an indie-pop kind of girl, but I wasn't really sure why—it wasn't like we'd ever discussed it.

I expected to find her studying, or working out or something, but instead she was curled up on the sofa with a textbook open under her arm as the music blared. If my ears hadn't felt like they were about to rupture it might have been cute, but as it was I scowled as I grabbed the controller from the coffee table and turned it down to a more bearable decibel. Bryn didn't even stir.

I watched her for a second, hesitating, before sighing and grabbing the bookmark she'd left on the floor and stuffing it inside the textbook as I pulled a blanket up over her. My phone vibrated in the back pocket of my skinny jeans and I reached for it as I snagged an unopened box of

Lucky Charms from the kitchen and headed to my room. I didn't look at it until my jeans had hit the floor, replaced with my PJs with the fluffy lining inside for optimal coziness. Then I froze.

One missed call. Dad.

I hadn't heard from them in *months* and now I had a missed call? My mind immediately focused on all the possibilities for why he would suddenly call now—was one of them sick? Dying? Or had it been a butt dial? I stared at the name on the screen for longer than was probably healthy before holding down the button on the side of my phone to turn it off. He would either call back, or he wouldn't. But I didn't want to give myself the temptation of checking it every five seconds, waiting for a call that might never come.

I laid back in bed, switching on the small bedside lap as I did so, and stared up at the ceiling. Bryn's music played softly through the walls as I tried to get my thoughts to stop churning—it didn't work. I couldn't help but picture the way my mom's olive skin had turned chalky white after St Agatha's had broken the news to her, or the way my dad's hands had grabbed the sides of his chair like he'd been about to go head first into freefall. It was their problem, not mine. I'd always been who I was, they just hadn't known about it until that moment. Or maybe they had, and were finally forced to confront it. Either way, it wasn't me who needed to change.

The longer I laid there, the more my thoughts swirled. Caught between the past and my present, worried for my future. Everyone seemed to have a *passion,* some idea of what they wanted to do or where they wanted to go, everyone except me. Jamie had her music and Bryn had the law, Ryan wanted to work in psychiatry or something and Kat... Well, I guess she was still figuring things out too, but she would be graduating soon so I had to imagine she was feeling almost as much pressure as me.

I didn't notice the sun going down outside of my window, didn't remember falling asleep. I must have reached to turn off the light at some point and by the time I was awake again my eyes had adjusted to the dark. I blinked, but the world didn't change. The backs of my eyelids were as endless as the room around me, no hints of shapes or vague outlines, just darkness that numbed the places inside I hadn't even realized were still sore.

A timid knock half-stirred me, bringing me back onto the cusp of the world as the sound seemed to ripple through the darkness. A moment passed, two, then the faint sound of retreating footsteps reached me. I eased back into myself, letting my mind fall silent once more until another, louder knock hit the wood of my door incessantly. I didn't respond.

A bright light seared through the room and I blinked repeatedly as my eyes watered. A silhouette walked towards me and I couldn't make out their face with the light behind them. The bed dipped as they sat down on the edge. *Jamie?*

"Get up." Bryn. I would have bit back my disappointment but found that I felt absolute, blissful nothingness.

"Why."

"Does it matter?"

"Where's Jamie?"

"Ryan's." Oh. Of course. "Get up. We're going to drink."

"I don't want to go out."

"Then we'll drink at home. You have tequila, right?"

I considered her words, a stirring of intrigue slowly trying to form inside me. "Why?" I asked again and Bryn seemed to go very still, like she wasn't even daring to breathe.

"Because you've been in your room for a full day and I'm worried."

That couldn't be right. A full day? Hadn't it just been early afternoon a second ago? "Can you just leave, please." I saw her shoulders slump but couldn't even bring myself to feel bad even though I wanted to. Of course, that was before she stood up and, quicker than I thought possible, ripped the sheets off of me.

"Hey!" I sat bolt upright and scrambled for them, trying to tug them back out of her hands. "What the hell are you doing?"

"I tried being gentle. You need to get up and get drunk with me."

"What if I'd been naked under there?"

For the first time I caught a glimpse of her blue eyes in the light making its way in through my open door. "Nothing I didn't already see a few nights ago."

It felt like the air between us became weighted at her words and I frowned. "Well, you didn't have to look."

"Trust me, I did my best."

I snorted, but relinquished the covers and let her drag me out into the hall where the light from the living room made me feel slightly nauseous. "Why are we drinking tequila again? Do you think I'll let you get in bed with me like last time?"

Bryn laughed as she rummaged in the kitchen and I flopped down onto the couch, pulling the soft blanket I'd used to cover Bryn earlier up and over my legs. Well, I'd thought it was earlier, but apparently not. *A full day.* How was my bladder not fit to burst right now?

As soon as I had the thought I realized it actually was and I had just been tuning it out while I disassociated or whatever had been happening. It wasn't something I'd experienced before, but the overwhelming feeling of both nothingness and hopelessness had been paralyzing. I ran to the bathroom and felt a lot more relaxed by the time I sat back down on the sofa and accepted the glass Bryn passed me.

"Talk," she said and I raised an eyebrow as I sipped my drink. It probably wasn't wise for alcohol to be the first thing hitting my stomach after I'd checked out, but there we were.

"About what?"

"Whatever made you stay in your room for nearly twenty-four hours straight."

"Seriously?" She shook her head and I sipped my drink again while I let my thoughts roam. "My dad tried to call me."

"Tried? You didn't answer?"

"I missed it, I was in a meeting. But I guess just seeing

his name brought up a lot of stuff for me on an already semi-shitty day."

Bryn reached over and took my drink from me, taking a long swallow before passing it back and I shook my head at her bemusedly. I guess being my roommate automatically made her the kind of friend I shared my drink with. "What happened?"

I reached for the controller for the TV Jamie and Ryan had recently mounted on the wall and scrolled aimlessly through my music for some background noise. "In my meeting? They might kick me off my course for not attending. And for not submitting my assignments."

Bryn nodded slowly as she stood and walked back into the kitchen, returning with the whole tequila bottle. "Sounds like we're going to need a little more alcohol for this."

I snorted but didn't deny it. She took a swig and winced before passing it to me.

"So why did you skip?"

"I just didn't want to go." When she raised an eyebrow at me dubiously I shrugged. "It feels like a waste of time. The only reason I'm here instead of St Agatha's is because they, and my parents, wanted to get rid of me. Not because I chose to be here."

"I'm sure they didn't—"

"They made sure I had access to my inheritance and essentially told me to have a nice life," I interrupted and she bit her lip. "What, you don't believe me?"

Her head snapped up and her blue eyes flashed with some unreadable emotion. "No. Of course I believe you.

I'm just *pissed* that anyone would do that to you, let alone your parents."

I blinked, not expecting for her to seem so... Well, mad. "It's okay."

"No." Bryn shook her head, her blonde hair swaying so that the smell of her shampoo wafted toward me. "No, it's not okay, Liv. You deserve so much better than that."

I wasn't sure what to say, so I sipped some more tequila from the bottle and looked away. "Thanks?"

Quiet settled between us, not uncomfortably, and we passed the bottle back and forth without a word until we both tried to speak at the same time.

"I just feel like everything I touch turns to shit, like all my decisions are the wrong ones—"

"I'm sorry if I made things weird when I moved in—"

We looked at each other, awkward chuckles spilling out of our mouths as I gestured for her to go first.

"I tried to say no to Jamie, I was going to stay with Kit and the boys, but she insisted and well..."

"There's not really any saying no to her once she's set her mind to something." I smiled and shrugged. "It's fine. You're tidier than Jamie, at least."

Bryn laughed. "And you leave the seat down, so really this is a win-win."

"Exactly." The room was starting to feel warm and a little fuzzy and when I looked at the bottle of tequila I realized why. "Holy crap, maybe we should chill out a little with that. Or," I said, re-considering, "maybe we should keep drinking and eat a pizza."

"Sounds like a plan. Want me to order?"

I nodded and she pulled out her phone, reminding me that mine had apparently been turned off for a while. "I'll be right back." I'd left it on my nightstand and it still had the majority of its battery when I powered it back on. No missed calls. A half-dozen messages from Kat, and Jamie had sent me a first recording of one of the new songs she was working on with Max, the record producer she'd signed with. Winters had sent me the details for an online lecture taster session that I decided to look at later, and that was it.

I locked it again and slumped back onto the sofa with Bryn as she finished setting up our delivery. Another perk of being in the center of things was that food tended to reach us pretty fast.

"Anything?" Bryn asked, nodding toward my phone, and I shook my head.

"Maybe he called me by mistake."

"Maybe," she murmured. "It's their loss either way."

"I guess." I swirled the golden tequila around the bottom of the bottle idly. "What about your parents? Were they... okay? With you?"

"My parents have always known, I wasn't exactly a shy kid. But yeah, they were fine with me and Kit."

"That's nice," I murmured and she smiled.

"It is. Kit's only a little younger than me, so having someone who genuinely understood was helpful too."

"I'm an only child."

"Well, you can borrow Kit whenever you like. Him and Leo seem better, so he's less moody now."

I chuckled. "Are they a thing?"

Bryn rolled her eyes. "No. But they should be. I think they're worried about ruining their friendship or something."

Well, that hit a little close to home. "I get that."

"Jamie, huh."

My mouth popped open and then shut again. "I'm that obvious?"

Bryn pulled a face. "Well, it was a slight giveaway when you kissed me but said her name."

Crap. I'd managed to block that out. "Um, right. Sorry."

A light knock on the door had my stomach grumbling, like it could sense that food was here, and Bryn stood to grab it. The two boxes were still hot and I made grabby hands for the one that was mine, lifting the lids to check and realizing we had virtually the same order except—

"Ugh. Why would you ruin a perfectly good pizza with peppers?"

Bryn sat back down with her pizza and happily bit into a pepper-heavy slice, groaning loudly. "You don't know what you're missing."

I wrinkled my nose. "Keep telling yourself that."

We finished the tequila bottle between us and I wheezed as Bryn finished telling me a story about the first time she'd made out with a girl and her mom had walked in on them and decided to lecture them on safe sex. They were fourteen.

"Well, better to get the talk than never have it all." I

winced, not having meant for that to come out quite as acidic. "I mean—"

"It's okay." She smiled at me. "So anyway, what's your plan?"

"With what?"

"I mean, there's not really anything you can or should do about your parents. But you do have two issues you can do something about."

"Oh?"

"Radclyffe."

I wrinkled my nose but nodded for her to go on.

"And Jamie."

I sighed. "There's nothing to be done about Jamie. She's happy and I'm happy she's happy."

"Do you actually believe your own bullshit?" Bryn laughed at the surprised look on my face. "You're miserable. Actual, genuine misery."

"Every decision I make just seems to make things worse—especially when it comes to romance."

"I don't know, the redhead from *Luscious* was pretty hot."

"She was, wasn't she," I mused. "But even that was a dumb move, I don't know what I thought going out and getting screwed would help."

"Well," Bryn said slowly, "you never actually did the screwing."

I could feel myself blushing as I pulled on an errant thread in my PJ bottoms. "Are you trying to get in my pants right now?"

Her bark of laughter was slightly offensive and I frowned.

"I'm sorry, but no. Let's not forget that you haven't showered in a day and a half *and* you're in love with someone else. If I made a play for you, Olivia," she leaned in close, her blue eyes dancing with amusement as one side of her mouth quirked up, "I'd be playing for keeps."

"Good to know," I said, strangely breathless. "You're obviously more clear headed than me about all of this. Maybe I should just let you be in charge of my life for a bit. Like a super hands-on life coach."

Bryn laughed. "Sure."

Except... That would be kind of amazing actually, to not have to worry about a million things or wonder if I was making the right choice. To have someone I trusted just... do my thinking for me. And I did trust Bryn, surprisingly. I didn't always trust easy, but there were some people you came across in life that just instantly matched your vibe, like their energy complemented your own, and it kind of felt like that being around her.

"No, really."

She stopped laughing. "What?"

"I want you to help me get over Jamie, and work out what to do about my course. And, I suppose just generally figure my crap out."

"Liv, you don't need me for that, you're perfectly capable—"

"I'm not," I said quietly. "It feels like everyday things fall apart a little more. Please, Bryn?"

She watched me with a tight expression on her face,

her mouth hard and her jaw clenched. "If we do this, we do it my way."

"Whatever you want," I said earnestly. "But I draw the line at breaking the law."

"I can work with that," she said, a slow grin spreading across her face.

God help us both. What the hell had I just suggested?

CHAPTER FOUR

"ABOUT LAST NIGHT..."

"It was stupid, right?" Bryn laughed. "It's okay, I understand if you want to call it off."

I adjusted my bag on my shoulder as Bryn folded up the comforter she was using on the sofa. Honestly, I wasn't sure why she didn't just take Jamie's room, other than the fact that it was usually a mess, because it wasn't like Jamie was around enough to use it lately.

"I shouldn't have asked, I guess I was just overwhelmed. But I did have fun, so thanks for taking my mind off of things."

Bryn straightened and smiled at me. "Anytime." I even thought she meant it.

"I'm going to meet Jamie and Kat at *The Box,* do you want to come?"

"I've got class." She ran a brush through her hair before tying it up in one of those lazy buns that were somehow ridiculously chic while she did her make-up. "But thanks."

I smiled wryly. I had class too, but that wasn't stopping me. "See you later then."

Bryn waved and then got back to applying her mascara in a tiny mirror she'd pulled out of her make-up bag. I couldn't help but find it funny that she was literally living in our living room and yet still made less mess than Jamie usually would have on a daily basis.

It was warm outside, though the sky looked like it was deciding whether or not to rain, and the air was thick enough that I had a light sheen of moisture on my skin by the time I got to the bar. Kat was already waiting in a booth near the back and I grabbed a strawberry milkshake from the bar before joining her.

She raised a delicately sculpted brow as I sat down. "No cocktail?"

"Drank too much last night."

"Jamie?"

"Bryn." I didn't like the knowing look that passed over Kat's face at the mention of her name. "It wasn't like that. We were just hanging out."

"Hey, hey, I said nothing." The slight smirk stayed on her face though and I rolled my eyes as I sipped at my shake.

"You know, these are pretty good. Maybe we should make our cocktail meet-ups milkshake meet-ups instead."

Kat snorted. "Maybe we can alternate as needed." Probably a good call. "Have you seen Jamie yet today?"

"Nope," I said, popping the *p* extra loud like I was so nonchalant about it. "I think she—"

"Hey!" Kat looked up and I swiveled around to see Jamie approaching us, a red glow to her cheeks that could have been from the heat outside if not for her freshly-mussed hair. "I'm sorry, I'm sorry, I know I'm late."

"You're fine, I just got here." I smiled and she relaxed as she slid into the booth on the side opposite me. "I listened to the recording you sent me, it's so good. How's it been working with Max?"

Kat perked up and I watched her in surprise. As far as I knew, they'd never really spoken so her sudden interest in Jamie's answer was intriguing at the very least. Or maybe it was just Kat's innate love of any kind of gossip.

"It's great," Jamie said, a small smile flirting with her mouth. I knew what she must be thinking, that it's great considering she almost passed up the opportunity out of her own sheer stubbornness. "I actually saw him earlier and we tried to write something together—it was terrible, but we had fun doing it."

"Well, do you know who else has been hanging out together?" Kat said, casting a sly glance in my direction and I opened my mouth to cut her off but she was too fast. "Liv and Bryn."

"Oh really," Jamie said, stretching the word out as she leaned in close to Kat and they waggled their eyebrows in tandem. "So it was a good idea that she moved in then?"

"She moved in?" Kat looked accusingly between the two of us. "Why am I always the last to find out these things?"

"That's entirely inaccurate and you know it," I said dryly and Kat pouted. "It's temporary, her place flooded and Jamie insisted she crash with us while the repairs are done."

"But you guys are hanging out now?" Was it me or did Jamie sound... jealous?

"Tequila and pizza. No biggie." It was a biggie. Whenever someone comes and pulls you out of a depressive spiral and plies you with booze, food, and company, it's a biggie.

"Tequila, huh." Kat narrowed her eyes at me. "Spill."

"Um, okay? We drank the bottle between us."

"No, I mean, *spill*. What happened? Did you kiss again?" Kat leaned forward eagerly and I shot her a look to *shut up* that she promptly ignored.

"*Again*? There's been multiple kisses?" Jamie looked between the two of us and I huffed out a sigh. "Now who's the one who never knows anything?"

"Kat kissed her too!" I blurted and Jamie's mouth dropped open.

"Fuck she's good, I mean how crazy does your sex appeal have to be to get even the straight girls to kiss you?" Jamie shook her head, a slight smile on her mouth. "Good for you, Kat. It's good to try new things."

For once, Kat clearly didn't know what to say and I laughed at the expression on her face before choking the sound off abruptly as I glanced at Jamie and really took in her appearance.

"Your shirt is on inside out." I knew my voice was cold, I knew it had no right to be. But it was hard to remember that when it felt like things were ripping and tearing inside of me in a spiral of anger and sadness. It was unfair, she was my friend, nothing more, but it felt like Ryan had come in and taken the first good decision I'd made for myself since leaving St Agatha's. I wished I could just pretend, just shove all the pain and frustration down or, better yet... *move on.*

I stood abruptly and the girls stared up at me with wide eyes as I dug out my phone and checked the time. I'd been here only fifteen minutes, tops, and it had taken under ten to walk here, so if I hurried...

"I have to go," I said as I shuffled out of the booth and stilled only when Jamie's warm hand caught mine.

"Wait, Liv. I'm sorry, I—" Her eyes looked suspiciously shiny and I softened, I hadn't meant to put this on her. It wasn't her fault that I'd taken our friendship and almost ruined it with long looks and tension.

"Hey, no. It's fine, you're fine! I just forgot I have to talk to Bryn about something and she's leaving for class soon..."

"It can't wait until after?" Kat's look was pointed and I could tell she was pissed that I was leaving our weekly drinks and gossip sesh but also that I'd upset Jamie, something that was usually nigh impossible to do.

"No," I tried to say as gently as I could. "It can't." I smiled before turning for the door and let it drop as I picked up my pace.

Maybe last night hadn't been a mistake at all, perhaps it was the best way out of this mess I'd created for myself. Usually alcohol made things more messy, but right now it felt like last night had been the opposite of that. Uncomplicated. Clear. I couldn't do this by myself.

I turned down the alleyway not far from the apartment at a near jog and let all pretenses fade once I was in our building, pounding my feet up the stairs and fumbling the key in the lock as I ran inside and threw my small bag down on the floor.

"Bryn? Are you still here?" God I was out of breath, I needed to start working out again ASAP. I thought back to the one yoga class I'd attended recently and cringed. Maybe I wasn't so desperate to exercise after all, even if Bryn and I were on good terms now.

There was no response to my call but I checked the living room just to be sure and found it empty, just the lingering smell of her perfume on the air. She'd left the blinds open, sunlight streaming in from our view overlooking the park, and I cursed as I spotted her walking through the green on her way to class. I'd literally just missed her.

I bit my lip as I watched her walk before making my decision. I headed back for the door and pulled it clumsily shut behind me as I ran for the stairs. There wasn't enough time for me to half-ass it now. I shrugged out of my light jacket as I ran out of the building, through the alley, and turned towards the park rather than in the direction of the bar, sprinting after her.

"Bryn!" She didn't hear me, but I was close enough to see her up ahead, walking at a calm pace like she'd left early to have a sweet stroll. If I'd thought the humidity was bad earlier, it was nothing compared to flat-out sprinting in it.

"Bryn," I panted and she turned around at the sound of my footsteps, looking both confused and alarmed as she stepped towards me and steadied me with her hands on my bare arms. I pulled away, not wanting her to feel just how sweaty I was right then and tried to talk through my heavy breathing. "I made—a mistake—"

"We already had this conversation," she said, brows furrowing as we resumed walking and I clutched my side against the powerful stitch that was working to steal my breath. "It's fine, we were both just drunk and stupid."

"No, no." I gulped down the air and could have cried when a light breeze swept over us. "I'm saying, I made a mistake calling it off. I need you."

Clearly not expecting me to say that, Bryn's mouth dropped open before she quickly snapped it shut. "Okay."

"Really?" Now I felt breathless for another reason. She was still willing to help me, and if I had any hope of figuring out who I was and what *I* wanted, then I was going to need some help. "Thank you!" I sprang forward and hugged her, which was doubly awkward as we were still walking and I was dripping with sweat. She laughed but held me at arm's length.

"Yes, yes, I know I'm the best." A sly look came across her face and I tensed, waiting to hear what she was about to say. "So I guess my first official command is that you get your ass to a gym. How else are you going to run away from your more tenacious admirers?"

We slowly started walking again as I rolled my eyes. "Okay, well, first, you're not just going to be the boss of me—"

Bryn tugged me to a stop and stepped in close. "Yes, I am."

I swallowed hard as her gaze devoured mine. "Fine, but I get veto powers."

She smirked. "If that makes you feel better."

"Secondly, run away? What?"

"You've never had to run away before?" I shrugged and she shook her head in apparent disbelief. "Don't worry, it was a lame joke. I just figured you would be beating people off of you."

Did she... Did Bryn think I was hot? I mean, sure she'd flirted with me in the past, but that just seemed more like a personality trait than anything serious.

"Right," I said vaguely and then stopped at the end of the pathway when she did. Oh. Class. "I'll, um, see you at home then?"

"Sounds good."

I waved as I turned, walking at a much more sedate pace than the wild run I'd maintained when I'd chased her down.

"Liv!" Bryn still stood in the same spot and I raised one hand in an air-borne shrug until she called out again. "Make a list!"

Screw this. I wasn't going to scream at her from half-way up the path. I pointed at my phone and then continued walking as I typed out a message.

Liv: A list of what?

· · ·

Bryn: All the things you've ever wanted to do.

It felt like Bryn was underestimating just how much stuff that might be, so I sent back a flood of question marks and then stared at her reply.

Liv: ?????

Bryn: Xoxo

I wasn't sure what making this list was going to accomplish, but I'd asked her to help me and I'd meant it. Now for both Jamie's sake and mine, I just had to hope this worked.

There was a soft breeze running through the air as I made the walk back to the apartment slowly, enjoying the feel of it cooling my sweaty skin. A few other college students walked past in the opposite direction to me, heading for campus, and I looked away awkwardly when one guy stared at me for a bit longer than was strictly comfortable.

By the time I got home, I was mostly dry and my breath only burned in my throat a little but I still took an extra puff of my inhaler just in case. Running in the heat was just not good for me.

I kicked off my shoes and stowed them neatly on the

rack by the door before moving into the living room and shrieking when I found Kat waiting for me.

"Holy shit! You scared me." I pressed a hand to my chest as I sucked down a breath. My poor heart was going through the ringer today. "What are you doing here?"

"I used the key," Kat said as she relaxed back against the gray fabric of the sofa.

"Okay," I said slowly and she threw me a look that made me wince. Great, she was mad. "Is everything, um, alright?"

"You tell me—you're the one who ran out of *The Box* like your ass was on fire."

"I had to—"

"Talk to Bryn, yeah. You said that already." Kat folded her arms across her chest as she locked me in her sights, green eyes glinting challengingly. "Did you really have to talk to her? Or were you just avoiding Jamie?"

"Both," I said honestly and Kat nodded for me to continue. "Okay, fine. I didn't tell you before because it's not a big deal, but I might get kicked off my course and I just don't know what to do with my life or what *I* want—because I never really had the chance to choose before, you know? And then my dad called and I stayed in bed for like an entire day and Bryn is going to make all my decisions from now on."

Kat's mouth was hanging open as I rambled and I clicked my own shut to give her a chance to process. When she said nothing a few moments later I cleared my throat as I hesitantly sat down next to her on the couch, it helped calm me a little—I felt less like I was being interrogated now that I was beside her instead of under a proverbial spotlight.

"When-when you say Bryn is going to make all of your decisions for you…"

I nodded. "She's in charge. But I have veto powers."

"And this is going to… help?"

"I hope so."

"How?"

I stared at the baby pink wall opposite us as I thought her question over. "I don't know. She told me to make a list of everything I've ever wanted to do."

"I don't see how this will fix anything," Kat said carefully and I saw nothing but concern on her face when I turned to her.

"Maybe it won't." I laughed but it sounded wrong. "But I need to do something, I don't want to feel like this forever."

She wrapped her arms around me, her curly hair brushing my chin as she patted my back. "Then it's worth a shot."

I tried for a smile as she pulled away. It really was. If Bryn could help me figure out what I wanted and help me get over Jamie at the same time, then I had to try.

"Though I'm a little offended that you chose Bryn to make all your decisions and not me." Kat pouted and I laughed.

"It was just a right time, right place, thing," I assured her and grinned when she inclined her head regally.

"I guess I forgive you then."

I smacked a kiss on her cheek as I stood to grab us

some drinks from the kitchen. "As if you could stay mad at me. Where did Jamie go, anyway?"

Kat snorted. "Where do you think? Back to Ry's. She's half-convinced you hate her so, like, talk to her or something. Soon."

"I will." I sighed as I passed her a soda. "Can you believe that even with all this mess going on and the trouble Jamie had with Aaron and Taylor, this is still the most drama-free my life's been since St Agatha's?"

We cracked open our cans and my eyes watered at the first sip of fizz.

"Seriously?"

"It didn't go over well when people inevitably found out I'd been... fraternizing with the teacher."

"Because you were gay?"

"Because they thought I had been cheating my grades." I considered, tilting my head as I took another sip of my drink. "And because I was gay."

"You don't talk about it much," Kat mused as she picked at a loose thread on the hem of her black vest top. I knew it was likely killing her that she knew so little about everything that had happened there, so I decided to throw her a bone.

"There's honestly not much to tell. She was young, only a few years older than me, and we liked each other. It wasn't love or anything like that, but it was just nice to have someone for longer than a fleeting moment, not just stolen kisses in the field behind my high school or a moment of weakness that led to regret."

Kat's eyes were heavy on my face and I chose to meet

her gaze long enough to let her know I was alright. "You don't have to be anyone's secret any more."

"I know." I smiled and it felt good.

"Are you going to call your dad back?"

I shrugged. "No."

"You're not curious about why he called?"

That was the difference between me and Kat—she had to know, but I knew that some wounds were better left to heal.

"I don't even know if he called on purpose and if he called back... I honestly don't know if I would answer."

Kat's eyes were soft as she watched me. "You're strong."

I blinked and busied myself with my drink. "I don't know about that. I don't feel strong. Not like Jamie."

She shrugged. "There's different kinds of strengths. Jamie just happens to be more abrasive."

I laughed and Kat smirked at me. "What's going on with you anyway? I feel like I've barely seen you recently."

"That's because you keep avoiding Jamie."

I looked at her sheepishly but didn't deny it and she rolled her eyes.

"Even so," I said, semi-defensively, "I hardly even see you at the bar at the moment. Are you working somewhere else or—"

"You probably just missed me," she said, a shade too fast and I hid my doubt behind a smile and a nod. Kat, the biggest gossip I knew, had a secret. I decided not to push the issue. When she was ready to talk, I'd be there.

CHAPTER FIVE

COCOA & RUM HAD PLACED LITTLE TABLES outside, complete with chic gray umbrellas and chairs so its patrons could sit out in the sun without dying of heatstroke—something I knew Bryn appreciated slightly more than me. With her fair skin, it was a wonder she hadn't already burnt. Though that probably had something to do with the twenty-minutes she'd spent slathering on sunscreen before we'd left. I kind of missed the AC inside actually, my thighs were sticking to my chair and I wondered whether Kit would give me staff discount if I went back inside to order a muffin. Anything for a moment of chilled air. The humidity was thick today, like breathing in soup, and I'd found my hand straying toward my inhaler more than once.

I looked longingly through the big glass window that made up *Cocoa & Rum's* front-facing wall and sighed. Bryn had insisted on sitting outside because it was 'such a nice day', and she wasn't wrong but I could feel several beads of sweat dripping uncomfortably between my breasts.

I'd made her the list, as requested, but she'd refused to look at it straight away, insisting I sleep on it to see if I could think of more to add. Truth be told, I had jotted down a couple of more adventurous things at about two in the morning after tossing and turning. But now I had to show her and I couldn't help feeling strangely nervous as I sucked down my iced coffee. I really hadn't had all that much to put down, my mind had gone blank the longer I spent trying to come up with things—I was kind of hoping Bryn would have suggestions.

"Let's have it then." Bryn didn't wait for me to protest, just grabbed the small piece of paper from my hands and scanned it quickly before nodding as if satisfied. She looked up at me, her serious blue eyes in strange contrast to the cheery white sundress decorated with cute cherries she had chosen to wear out. The neckline was a sweetheart scoop and I had to work surprisingly hard to keep my focus from dropping too low. Anyone likely would have had the same problem, Bryn was stunning and that was just a fact. I probably looked like a slob in comparison—it was too hot today for me to care about make-up or pretty dresses, so I had thrown on my most lightweight pair of shorts and a strappy cotton cropped top with sneakers when Bryn had told me we were going out. It didn't help that she'd given me approximately ten minutes notice.

I sniffed and nearly sneezed as I caught the scent of pollen, at least there hadn't been any bugs trying to jump inside my coffee. That was another reason why I typically avoided sitting outside when I had food or drink to hand.

"So? What do you think?"

"All do-able," Bryn said, watching me over the rim of her red sunglasses.

I bit my lip. "All of them?"

Was that a hint of a smirk on her mouth? "Yep."

I tried not to think about item number four on the list and failed. *Skinny dipping. All do-able.* "Well, we don't have to do all of them—"

Bryn shook her head at me and I cut my words short. Right. Pushing boundaries, loving life, yada yada.

"Fine," I muttered and she grinned. "Why did we have to do this here?"

"Because I'm trying to build up a tan and," she looked over my shoulder and interest lit her eyes as she pushed her sunglasses up into her hair, "you need practice."

Practice? I had a bad feeling about where this was headed. "Bryn—"

"Not in charge," she reminded me and I sighed but relented. "There's a blonde girl two tables behind you sitting by herself. Go and get her number."

"What? No."

"Scared?"

"*No.*"

"Then do it. She's cute and you need to remember that other girls exist beyond Jamie."

"I know that." I tried to keep the defensiveness out of my voice and did a poor job as Bryn cocked a brow.

"Oh? When was the last time you went on a date? Or sexted?"

"*Sexted?*"

I'd known it was a mistake to say the last aloud when Bryn leaned forward excitedly. "Add it to the list."

"No."

"Adding it," she mouthed as she snagged a pen from somewhere inside her purse—why she carried one around was beyond me. The only thing I kept in my purse was an inhaler for emergencies, my phone, my ID, and some cash.

"If you're that desperate for me to date, why haven't *you* asked me out?" I mused and wished I hadn't asked when most of Bryn's cheer evaporated, her hand pausing above the paper before she set it down without writing anything.

"Generally I kind of prefer the girls I like to like me back." She shot me a dry look and I tried not to cringe. "So as a rule, I don't date girls who are in love with someone else. Bad for my ego. Plus, I don't want to be anyone's second choice."

I looked at her, alarmed. "I didn't mean—"

"I know. Now stop stalling and go and ask your girl out."

I stood reluctantly but was relieved to see an amused smile turning up the corners of her lips before I walked away. *Get her number.* This wouldn't be that hard, surely. Unless she wasn't into girls... that would make things pretty difficult.

I cleared my throat lightly as I approached the girl, her

blonde-white hair shining in the sunshine and pulled up into a high-pony. "Hey."

She swiveled to look at me and my mouth went dry. Crap.

"Oh. Hi. Need more pills?"

Of all the people Bryn could have picked for me to ask out, she'd managed to find the only one that had ever sold me drugs.

"Um." Oh God, what should I say? That my friend sent me over to ask her out but sorry, I didn't realize you were my drug dealer? Should I just buy some drugs to make it less awkward? I could feel the heat in my face growing and sincerely wished that the earth would open and swallow me whole. "I, um—"

I turned around without another word and walked quickly back over to the table where Bryn sat, an alarmed look on her face at whatever expression I now wore.

"What the hell happened?" she whisper-shouted as I tucked in my chair as quickly as possible. Maybe the woman behind us didn't care and just figured I was a weirdo, but my imagination told me eyes were boring into my back anyway.

"We need to leave," I said through clenched teeth. "Now."

"Liv, it can't have been that bad—"

My chair made a loud screech against the pavement as I stood. "*Now.*"

To her credit, Bryn didn't argue again—just quickly tucked in her chair and let me lead the way down the path through the park at what was probably a ridiculous pace until she grabbed a hold of my arm and tugged me to a stop.

"What happened? Was she rude to you?" Bryn looked back in the direction we'd fled from like she was about to storm the coffee shop and give that girl a piece of her mind. I quickly shook my head.

"You tried to set me up with my drug dealer."

"I—what?" Bryn closed her eyes and opened them again slowly, like that might help her process the words that had just come out of my mouth. "Since when do you have a drug dealer?"

"Since I went to *Luscious* and bought a pill for the first time ever—So now I'd go to her for drugs, not a date!"

Bryn folded her arms across her chest and my gaze dropped for just half a second. "Drug dealers are people too, you know."

"Sure, but that doesn't mean I want to date one."

Her lip twitched. "Think of the discounts."

I shook my head but couldn't stop the smile spreading across my face anyway. "You're ridiculous."

"You love it."

I kind of did. Bryn was a very different kind of friend than Kat, Jamie, or anyone else I'd had before. It felt like we were in our own little club, one the rest of the world and its problems couldn't infringe on in the way that they did when I was with the other girls.

"So what's next?" I asked, mainly to stop the strange track my thoughts had spiraled down. "Obviously that didn't work out, but I won't hold it against you too much."

Bryn turned slowly, threading her arm through mine as we started walking back in the direction of the apartment. "Exposure therapy."

I grimaced. "That doesn't sound fun." She steered me clear of the path once there was a break in the trees and flopped down onto the grass to sit in the sunshine. "You're going to get grass stains on your dress," I protested and she waved away my words as I sat down beside her.

"We'll try the whole date thing again another time, for now let's focus on your list and finding the things that *you* enjoy."

That didn't sound too bad. Part of the reason I struggled to know what I wanted out of life was probably because I'd never been allowed to explore it, or find my own way. I didn't have a bad childhood by any stretch of the imagination, but my parents were controlling—suffocating me in a way that I now realized was just as damaging as anything else.

"Though there are a couple of things I want to add that I think will help you with your... existential crisis." I snorted but waved for her to continue. "Okay, first, you're coming back to yoga with me. Tonight. You need to get out of the house more."

I didn't reply, too distracted by the huge, fluffy dog running towards us at full pelt before its owner called it back. Bryn nudged me with her foot and I refocused, my smile fading.

"Fine, fine."

Bryn nodded. "And I want you to try and find a new hobby."

That was probably the vaguest thing I've ever heard. "What about yoga?" I whined and she threw me a look that made me widen my eyes innocently.

"A *new* hobby. I know that wasn't your first class."

Had she been watching me?

"Are you at least going to try these new hobbies with me?"

"No," she said gently, tilting her head up to the sky to soak in the sun. "You have to do some things by yourself, Liv. I can't tell you who to be or who you are, that's for you to figure out."

"Where do you get all this wise-crap?"

"I've had too much therapy in my life to not pick up a few things." She eyed me shrewdly, squinting past her eyelashes. "You should consider going."

"Noted," I said dryly and she grinned. "And the 'exposure therapy' you mentioned?" I almost didn't want to ask.

"You're going to hang out with Jamie, and Jamie and Ryan." The expression on my face clearly let Bryn know what I thought about this plan. "You need to be around them and see them together without feeling bad about it. Jamie is your friend, so let's just get you used to being around them instead of avoiding them like the plague all the time."

I nodded reluctantly. "I guess that makes sense."

"Think of it like... Drinking hot coffee after you already burned your mouth, it might sting but eventually you'll stop feeling the burn."

"Deep."

"I've got a lot of bullshit analogies stored in here," she said, tapping the side of her head as we watched a car on the other side of the park drive past way too fast

I snorted. "All that therapy... It explains why you're so creepily well-adjusted."

"Thank you." She grinned as she tilted her head back toward the sky. "Have you heard anything more from your course leader?"

"Not really." I wrinkled my nose and held my breath against a sneeze as the pollen drifted up. "I've been trying not to think about it."

"Have you been to class at all since you spoke to them?"

"Nope," I said, wincing, and Bryn didn't reply. I peeked up at her, wondering if I would find disapproval on her face but instead found the opposite.

"Good. There's no point investing your time in something that you hate." She smiled slightly as she watched me. "You seem surprised I'd say that."

"Well, you just seem so... studious."

"I enjoy learning and I'm excited to be a lawyer. You don't know what you want to do yet, but I have full faith that you'll throw yourself into it one-hundred-percent once you figure it out. You should take her up on her offer of the taster sessions though, another class might be better."

Hearing that somehow relaxed me. Even though I knew I wasn't getting anything out of my course right now, I still felt guilty for skipping, for defying expectations. It was hard to shake the feeling that doing what *I* thought was right might somehow be a disappointment to others.

"Is that a command?" I teased and Bryn sat up straight.

"You bet your ass it is."

"I'm willing to try," I said, and it was true. But I was pretty sure that I was done with academia, it wasn't the subject so much as the institution at this point.

I laid back against the grass beside Bryn and sighed as the sun warmed my skin. "This has been a good day."

"Even though I made you ask out your drug dealer?"

I chuckled. "Even though you made me ask out my drug dealer."

"I'm glad you asked me to help you, Liv."

"Me too."

We were quiet for a few minutes, just listening to the breeze rustle the leaves in the trees and the footsteps of the people walking past, until our phones dinged simultaneously.

"Group message?" I wondered aloud, too lazy to check my cell and instead waiting for Bryn to catch me up.

"Yeah. Jamie's having a party at Ryan's."

Crap. It wasn't her birthday, was it? "What for? And why wouldn't she just have it at ours?"

"Doesn't say."

I made a non-commital noise. "I guess it saves us the clean up."

"Wise."

I laughed. "It's not her birthday, right?"

"I have no clue but, knowing Jamie, if it was she would undoubtedly have been reminding us for weeks."

"True," I allowed. "When's your birthday?"

"Why, you going to buy me something pretty?"

"Maybe."

"It's November seventeenth."

"Winter baby."

"Yeah, Kit was born in the spring."

For some reason it felt like that fit, he was always bursting with color and that was what Spring-time was for me. "Mine's March third, in case you want to return the favor."

"Wow, free advice and now pretty presents... You're more high maintenance than my last girlfriend."

I sat upright and threw a bundle of the grass I'd pulled out of the ground at her. "Someone wanted to date you? I'm shocked."

"That's because the only time we were in bed together, we were asleep." Bryn smirked and sat up too and I opted to ignore her comment with a laugh, feeling almost breathless as we stood to head home.

"When's this party then?"

"Friday."

Great. Practically a whole week for me to obsess over it before it happened. "I'm guessing I can't sit this one out?"

"Exposure therapy," she reminded me and I sighed. I'd figured she would say that.

"Okay, I can admit that wasn't the worst thing in the world," I said breathlessly to Bryn as we left the yoga studio and the cool night air hit us. I'd actually missed yoga, the deep breathing exercises often helped to calm my mind and despite it being dark out for the walk home I felt relatively relaxed. It was amazing how much more pleasant the experience had been when I wasn't suffering from a ridiculously bad hangover or crushing embarrassment.

Bryn lowered her water bottle and smiled, her skin glowy and flushed from the exercise. I was probably going to hurt a lot tomorrow, and for the next few weeks until I got back into shape, but I didn't mind too much. It was good to get out of the apartment and do something I'd once found a lot of comfort and control in.

"I, um, got something for you." Bryn dug in her jacket pocket and handed over a small card. It was cream and a name was emblazoned across a large diamond-geometric design. I raised an eyebrow.

"You're giving me the name of your therapist?"

"I don't see her anymore. I found someone new when I moved here from Cali, but she does video calls now so I thought maybe..."

I pocketed the number and nodded as we continued walking past the mall, across the road, and into the park. "Thanks." I appreciated the thought, especially because I knew it was well-intentioned and not some kind of manipulation—a test of 'weakness', like it would have been if my parents had suggested it. "How did you get into all the therapy stuff anyway?"

"My mom loves it. As soon as I hit my teens she got me to sit down a couple times a month with a therapist—Mr Calloway," she said, smiling fondly and I watched her in quiet fascination as we passed under a street light.

Footsteps sounded behind us and I moved half a step closer to Bryn, slowing our pace so that whoever was there could overtake us while we stayed inside the vicinity of the light.

It wasn't until the footsteps slowed too that I tensed up. Bryn noticed and glanced behind us, her jaw tight when she turned back around.

"Hey beautiful," a voice called from behind us and I let my pace pick up a little.

"Just ignore him," Bryn said quietly, "and he'll lose interest."

I nodded absently, my heart thumping too hard in my chest and pins and needles pricking painfully in my arms as my adrenaline surged.

"I was talking to you," the guy continued, jogging forward to walk on the other side of Bryn and swiftly backing away as we approached the end of the park and busier part of town.

"Liv!"

I jumped, a gasp falling out of my mouth and I waved frantically when I realized who was standing outside of *The Box.*

Xander crossed over to us quickly, his eyes on the retreating figure of the man who'd been heckling us as he turned in the direction of the college campus rather than coming into town. "Everything okay?"

My breaths were coming unevenly but I nodded as I wrangled my panic back under control. Bryn blew out a slow breath before she looked at me and I could see the concern in her eyes.

"Maybe we'll do the morning class."

I nodded, still a little shaky, as I managed a wobbly smile for Xander. "What're you doing out here?"

He nodded down to the cigarette in his hand and I wrinkled my nose as the smell hit me. "I was just having a quick smoke when I saw you. What did that guy want?"

"Ah, nothing. The usual."

The frown on his face in response to my words finally made my heart slow as it sank in that I was with Xander and he wouldn't let anything bad happen to us.

"Do you want me to walk you back home?"

I shook my head. "It's alright, we're practically there now."

"I don't mind," he protested, pushing a stubborn strand of dark hair back and out of his eyes. "I'm always happy to walk you guys home."

I loved that he didn't hesitate to include Bryn in that offer, though he likely knew her better than I did considering he was friends with her brother.

Bryn pressed a quick kiss to his cheek and threaded her arm through mine. "We'll text you as soon as we get back."

He nodded and watched reluctantly as we walked away until I waved him back inside.

"You okay?" Bryn asked quietly as we walked the short distance to Jamie's.

I shrugged. "I guess."

She smiled, her face illuminated yellow by the cheap lights in the communal hall as we tugged open the metal door that led up to the apartment. "Same." We trudged up the stairs, adrenaline plus yoga making us more tired than we otherwise would have been as we pushed into the apartment.

My hands unclenched at the sight of the familiar red walls. Home. *Safe.*

I walked to the kitchen and gulped down a glass of cold water before heading to my room and shucking off my workout clothes. When I came back out of my room, Bryn was waiting in the living room in her pajamas... vodka bottle in hand.

"You were out of tequila," she said as she grimaced at the clear liquid.

I sighed as I took it from her. That sounded about right. "We'll make do," I said, choking a little as I sipped and passed the bottle to her.

"When life gives you lemons..." she muttered as she took her own swig.

"...make margaritas," I quipped and Bryn snorted, vodka trickling out of her nose.

CHAPTER SIX

My closet was full of clothes and yet, I had nothing to wear. Maybe I was just being too picky. 'Totally-not-in-love-with-you' was a hard vibe to pin down and 'Everything-is-fine' was an even harder message to broadcast with a mini skirt.

Bryn knocked on my door and I ignored her. It was the third time she'd knocked to make sure I was actually getting ready and not trying to skip this party. As much as I would have liked to do just that, Bryn and Kat had been right—I couldn't just keep avoiding Jamie forever in the hopes that I would miraculously stop loving her. I needed to be proactive.

I sighed, reaching for a square-necked red dress and climbing into it just as my bedroom door flew open.

"Oh good, you're getting dressed."

"Come in," I muttered sarcastically and Bryn smirked as she sat on the edge of my bed while she watched me pick out my make-up. "Is there a reason you're sitting in here?"

Of course, Bryn was already done and set to leave. Her blonde hair fell in glossy waves and her top was off-the-shoulder and in a shade of blue that perfectly matched her eyes. I avoided looking in the mirror, refusing to second-guess this dress I'd picked out again. Instead, I slicked on some mascara and some red lip gloss, dusted on some highlighter, and grabbed some chunky heels from the floor of my closet.

"Are you nervous?"

I shot Bryn a look. "You know, most people wouldn't consider a closed door an invitation."

"Yeah, well, I figure I'm the one in charge so..."

I rolled my eyes. "You've gone mad with power."

Bryn laughed and I couldn't help but join in. She stood and smoothed down her white denim skirt. In her beachy heeled sandals, I had to crane my head to look at her face.

"You know, I'm pretty sure nobody will notice if I don't go," I tried and didn't resist when Bryn took my arm in hers and tugged me out of my bedroom and into the hall. "I'll take that as a *no*."

Getting ready with Bryn just reminded me of the time Jamie had taken me to my first frat party. We'd gotten dressed up together then too and before we'd left, she'd pressed her purple lips to my cheek and I'd thought about it all night even as she successfully made her ex jealous by dancing with and generally being all over Ryan. I touched my cheek absently before grabbing a light jacket and following Bryn out the door.

It seemed odd to me that Jamie was hosting the party at Ryan's, seeing as it used to be the house he shared with her ex (and her ex's brother and best friend) until he'd been suspended for doing drugs. But that was Jamie all over, I supposed, laughing in the face of anything bad as she dared the world to fuck with her.

It was still light out, so we chanced the walk through the park that sat in the middle of town, connecting the campus to the shops. A lady who looked vaguely familiar was out walking her dog, a tiny little puppy, and I cooed at it as it jumped up at me and I buried my hands in its thick, curly fur.

"You like dogs?"

I looked up at Bryn, jumping a little, so absorbed in the puppy I'd sort of forgotten she was there. "Love them. Never had time for one before and my mom wouldn't be caught dead with an animal in the house." I rolled my eyes as I smiled at the puppy's owner before standing up out of my crouch. "What a sweetheart."

"Oh, don't be fooled—she's a handful!"

We laughed and Bryn and I walked on as I sent wistful glances back behind us.

"I bet Jamie wouldn't mind if you got one."

"What?" I furrowed my brow. "No, I couldn't."

"Why not?"

I didn't have an answer to that question really, because there wasn't one. It was just a habit, like this was still something forbidden. Sure, I hadn't been allowed a pet in the past, but I was a grown woman now and money wasn't an issue thanks to the inheritance I'd gained when I'd turned eighteen.

I stayed quiet, letting the idea sit at the back of my brain as we made it out the other end of the park and walked up to Ryan's door.

Leo opened it, his brown eyes going wide for a second when he saw us standing there poised to knock. "Oh, sorry." He said nothing else, just stepped back and held it open.

"Thanks," I said, smiling lightly as I stepped inside to the sound of music and laughter.

Bryn stopped to talk to him and I hovered awkwardly, not wanting to intrude on their conversation but also unwilling to walk into the room without Bryn at my side. Leo stepped out of the door, vape in hand, and Bryn and I made our way through the sparse hallway and into the living room.

I'd never been there before, but it was relatively clean though it was a bit bare. Jamie was curled up on the worn leather couch with Ryan, a red cup in her hand as she laughed, and I fought back the pang of longing as I looked away. Crap. We were one of the first people here.

Jamie turned to us and her eyes lit up. "Liv! You're here!"

I tried not to wince at the genuine surprise in her voice. God I'd been flaky lately. "Of course, I couldn't miss... whatever this is."

"It's a listening party," Ryan said smoothly, his eyes

warm as he settled a hand on Jamie's bare thigh. "Jamie's first song with Max's label has its first release today."

"Oh wow." I smiled and tried to inject as much cheer in it as possible while I watched Jamie lean into Ryan and kiss him. "I'm just going to—" I turned around, hurrying in the same direction Kit had gone in to get a drink. Maybe two.

"Baby steps," Bryn murmured and I ignored her, instead focusing on the shot she was pouring me.

Commotion from the hall had me looking up hopefully, desperate for a distraction, and relief washed through me when I spotted Xander's tall form—always coming to my rescue.

I hurried out, drink in hand, not really sure what Bryn had poured for me and not caring as the tingle of the vodka shot began to kick in.

"Xander!" I said cheerfully and then had to work to keep my smile in place when I realized who he was talking to. "Ryan," I said evenly and his dimples flashed at me when he grinned. "What's up?"

"Oh, nothing, we were just talking about basketball. Since the football season is pretty much over and I'm going to be here all summer, it's nice to have something to keep me busy besides Jamie."

I tried not to think about all the ways Jamie would be keeping him busy, and succeeded when Bryn nudged me with a pointed glance. Xander looked between us, a quirk to his brows that spelled trouble. He had a bad habit of seeing both too much and too little, so there was no way to know what conclusions he was drawing.

"Do you like to play, Liv?" he said, and Ryan raised his eyebrows as he waited for my answer.

"Ah, it's not really—" Bryn nudged me again, harder this time, and I shot her a glare as I changed my reply. "Not really something I'd considered, but I'd love to if you'll have me."

Bryn beamed and I rolled my eyes. So this was about this list, trying a new hobby and some exposure therapy with Ryan at the same time. I'd bet she was feeling smug about the efficiency of this set-up, and one glance at the smirk curling her pink lips confirmed that to be true.

"Of course! We usually play on Tuesday afternoons, does that work for you?"

"Sure," I said begrudgingly and Ryan smiled.

"Can't wait," he said and I tried to make my grimace look happier.

"Come on," I muttered as I dragged Bryn away, otherwise who knew what she'd have me agreeing to do next.

"How long do I have to stay here again?" I muttered to Bryn as I headed for the boys' kitchen for a refill. Compared to the football parties the team hosted, this was a relatively quiet affair with just our group, music and drinks. I found myself grateful it wasn't Jamie's birthday, that would undoubtedly have been a rowdier affair.

Instead we were celebrating the first finished recording she'd done with Max at the Sun City label. Apparently her song was being soft-launched on social media, whatever that meant, but she'd been both super excited and super drunk when she'd tried to explain it to me.

I'd been here almost two hours now and was pleasantly buzzed thanks to Xander—he poured his drinks *strong*. I'd even managed to forget about the standing date I now had with him and Ryan to play basketball, of all things.

I'd sat with Jamie and Ryan for a full five minutes on the four-seater couch and hadn't burst into flames, so that was a good sign, but I couldn't exactly say I was having a good time either. Bryn had spent the majority of the night talking in the corner of the room with her brother and Leo, while shooting meaningful glances at me whenever I spent too long avoiding Jamie. Though I had a welcome reprieve when Nick, one of Jamie's history coursemates, showed up and the attention was diverted by her happy squeal. We'd joked around together when we'd first met that he was Jamie's other gay, Black friend—it was an interesting category to be thrown into. Though the 'friend' part was the part that stung. But it was now a running joke between me and Nick whenever we saw each other.

"My other half," he announced as he spotted me lurking off to the side and pressed a quick kiss to my cheek. "How're things?"

"Not too terrible," I quipped and he smirked.

"A ringing endorsement for life."

"I try," I said dryly. "Where have you been lately? I don't think I've seen you at the apartment for a couple weeks."

"Just busy, work, class..." A smile tugged at his mouth and made his already-gorgeous midnight-face stunning. "I met someone."

"Must be something in the air," I said, nodding at Jamie and Ryan snuggling in the corner. "How'd you meet?"

"He's actually a family friend I hadn't seen in years."

"Ah, young love then." I smiled and he chuckled.

"Kind of. What about you? Seeing anyone new?"

I was saved from answering by the arrival of Max and, oddly enough, Kat and I raised an eyebrow at her as she walked past. Had they come together? Or just met up on the way in?

"Is it live?" Jamie's cheeks were flushed, probably from a mix of alcohol and excitement, her dark eyes glittered and her mouth was slightly swollen from Ryan's kisses and I could feel the alcohol sour in my stomach.

"It is." Max kept his face blank before letting a smile break out. "It's trending."

"Holy shit, you're kidding me."

"I'm so proud of you," I heard Ryan murmur and it felt like a fist tightening around my heart as I worked to keep my smile in place.

Max was practically glowing with pride, his tanned skin making him look more like a surfer than a record producer, except for the odd smudge of pink at the edge of his white collar...

I narrowed my eyes on Kat's perfect, pink coated mouth. When she decided to fess up, it was going to be good I could tell.

I slunk outside as the music was turned up a little louder, Max insisting on playing Jamie's new song—I just needed a second to breathe.

The music was muffled outside the boys' house and I sat down on the steps leading up to their porch to take in the night air. It was surprisingly cool out, like maybe we'd have rain, and I shivered as I looked up at the sky. There were a few stars, but mostly there was too much city pollution for us to see them that well and for a second it made me miss the quietness of my home town. The door opened and someone sat down beside me. I looked up in surprise, expecting Bryn but instead finding her brother.

"Hey."

"Hi."

I laughed quietly as the silence overtook us again. "Needed some space?"

"Yeah, I guess. Plus I wanted to talk to you."

There was that seriousness again, it felt out of place on Kit's face. "What's wrong?"

He paused before his eyes, so much like his sister's, met mine. "I don't know what you and Bryn are up to together, and I don't need to know, but she's softer than she pretends, Liv. Don't hurt her."

"It's not like that. We're just friends."

Kit nodded and then ran his pale hands through his shock of blue hair, mussing it up. "Just be careful, okay? I like you, Liv. But she's my sister, she comes first."

I smiled slightly. For the first time, I kind of wished I'd had a brother or sister. "I get it."

The door opened behind us and I glanced over as light from the hall escaped and Bryn stepped out, seeming surprised to see her brother there.

"Everything alright?"

Kit stood up and kissed Bryn on the cheek as he passed her to walk back inside. I understood his protectiveness, the two siblings certainly seemed close. It was something I found myself jealous of, despite the relief that came with knowing that I was the only person who'd been subjected to my parents' terrible excuse for parenting. I glanced at Bryn beside me and found her already watching me.

I'd thought she'd give me crap for leaving, but instead she said, "You did good."

"Really? It feels like the opposite."

Bryn shrugged. "Sometimes it's hard to do the thing that's right for you."

"Does that mean that I can go home, then?"

Her eyes ran over my face before she said, "If that's what you really want, then sure."

I thought it over and shook my head. I wanted to be inside, having a good time with my friends and getting a little drunk. What I really wanted was to not feel this way any more. "You know, sometimes I wish I could be a little more like her. Jamie, I mean. Care a little less, do my own thing without giving a crap about the expectations or consequences."

"That's not who you are," Bryn said quietly. "You

care, deeply, and that's not a bad thing. Except when you fall, you fall hard."

"I'm my own worst enemy."

"Maybe." She shrugged. "But you'll be okay."

I hadn't realized how much I'd needed to hear those words until just then, and Bryn reached out to squeeze my hand like she understood.

"Ready to go back in?"

I squared my shoulders and pasted on a smile. "Only if you promise to get me very, obnoxiously, drunk."

"That, I think I can do."

CHAPTER SEVEN

"You know, you're a real cover hog."

Bryn tucked her arm under her head and looked me dead in the eye. "I make no apologies."

I couldn't remember the last time a friend had spent the night in my bed, maybe when I was ten and my best friend at the time wanted to do a slumber party—it turned out to be a lot less fun than she was expecting, I think. My mom had made us get in bed by seven, provided a 'midnight snack' at seven-thirty that consisted of cucumber sandwiches and crackers, and then I'd been forbidden from doing anything like that again because my mom had found it 'too stressful'.

Last night had been so completely different from that experience, I kind of wanted to cry. It wasn't something I'd even considered adding to my list, but I wished I'd thought of it. We'd got back from Jamie's party at about two in the morning, both drunk but it was the good, giggly kind. I'd immediately flopped into bed and Bryn had been horrified, insisting I 'get my ass up' and take off my make-up with her. That led to a five-step skin-care routine and eating cake in bed before we both crashed from the sugar high and fell asleep chatting about nothing.

"Do you have plans today?" Bryn asked, pulling me out of my thoughts and instantly setting me on edge. There was nothing wrong with the question itself, but for some reason it triggered the same kind of anxiety I got when somebody says *Can I ask you something?*

"No... Why?"

"Well, it's not on your list. But from everything you've told me so far about how you grew up and, well, just from observing you to be honest, I want us to do something."

"Okay?"

"Duvet Day."

"I'm listening." I relaxed back against the mound of pillows as I rolled on my side to look at her.

"We stay in bed all day. You're allowed to leave to pee, get snacks, and that's it."

I frowned a little. "What about showering?"

"Nope."

"But what are we going to do in bed all day?"

The twitch of Bryn's lips told me she had a dirty response to that question but was holding it in. "Movies. We're going to watch all the classics."

Why did I get the feeling that my idea of classics would be very different from Bryn's?

"I'm down. What, exactly, is this supposed to be teaching me though? Or are you just looking to spend some more time in a real bed before you have to go back on the sofa?"

Bryn laughed. "Your sofa is surprisingly comfortable actually. Plus, you snore. The lesson here is that not everything has to be a lesson. You don't have to be *on* all the time. Just take the day, chill out."

"Like, self-care?"

"Yep." The smug look on her face made me laugh and I snuggled deeper into my pillow.

"Fine, consider me ready to relax." I pointed out my laptop to her so we could load up a movie and couldn't help my giggle as I saw her choice. "*Legally Blonde?* Is this why you wanted to be a lawyer?"

"It's always been my dream to say *ammonium thioglycolate* in court, that moment changed me for life."

We laughed together and I had to admit the movie was better than I remembered, though Reese Witherspoon's attraction to Emmett always escaped me.

"His head is shaped like a penis," I protested and Bryn choked on her soda, coughing violently as she laughed.

"You did not just say that."

"I mean, he had a nice personality, but so do a lot of guys whose heads aren't quite so... phallic."

"Oh my god." Bryn wheezed as she tried to control her laughter, her face bright red and her eyes wet. "The crap that comes out of your mouth."

I grinned and shrugged. "I can't believe I forgot Alaric is in it."

"Al-a-whoo?"

I went very still. "Bryn."

"Yeah?"

"This is an important question."

She suddenly looked nervous, worrying her lip between her teeth as she nodded.

"Have you not seen *The Vampire Diaries*?"

She slapped my arm. "Seriously? That's what you wanted to ask me?"

"I'm going to need you to answer right now."

She snorted. "No."

"No, as in, you haven't not seen it? Or no, as in, you've not-not seen it?"

Bryn's eyes went distant. "I think you just broke my brain."

"I thought you were studying the law? Shouldn't you be used to over-complicated language describing things that could easily be simplified?" I laughed when she mimicked her mind exploding. "Well, I'm about to make you feel things."

"Oh, do tell." Her smile was wolfish and I snorted.

"Yeah, joke all you like. You just wait until you're hooked on this show and then you get to the end of season two."

"What happens at the end of season two?"

"Emotional damage."

I hit play on episode one and we giggled at the clothes and clunky cell phones as I tried to reassure her that all pilot episodes are crappy and that the show was worth sticking with.

Before I knew it, it was nine in the evening and we were mid-way through season two.

"Okay, we should stop here."

"What? Why?" Bryn whined and I couldn't help the smugness that swelled. I'd *told* her she'd like it.

"We need fortification before we watch the last few episodes."

"Okay...?"

"You order some food. I'll go and grab some tissues."

"Oh damn," she said and I nodded slowly. Shit was about to get real. "I wanted to ask you something actually, it's fine if you say no." Now it was my turn to be anxious again and she laughed when she saw my face. "Relax. It's not serious. I got an email yesterday afternoon that I can go and check out my place, see if anything else is salvageable. I was wondering if you'd come with me?"

"Sure," I said easily. "Do we need Kit or anyone in case there's stuff to carry?"

"I don't think there's going to be much, but we can always call him when we get there if there is."

I nodded. "Sounds good to me." I pointed sternly at her. "Now order us some comfort food to get through these last few episodes."

"Yes, ma'am."

For some reason, the words sent a hot shiver over my skin and I walked away before Bryn could see and ask me about it because, honestly, I wasn't sure what I would say.

I stopped in the hall on my way to the bathroom as someone knocked on the door and nearly tripped answering it on an errant heel one of us had left lying around after we'd got home last night.

"Hey." I leaned against the door and then quickly stepped back as Kat bustled past me. "What's up?"

She seemed agitated, her hair a mess like she'd been running her hands through it, and two spots of color were visible on the high points of her cheeks. "Nothing."

"Okay," I said slowly as I closed the door. "Um, you want to hang out?"

"What?" She blinked her green eyes like she barely even registered I was there before she nodded. "Oh, yeah. Sure."

I snorted. Only Kat. "We're watching TVD."

That caught her attention, but for the wrong reasons. "*We*?"

"Bryn and me. She's never seen it before."

As if saying her name had summoned her out of thin air, Bryn poked her blonde head out around my bedroom door and quirked an eyebrow when she saw Kat. "Oh, hey! You want pizza?"

"God, yes. Put everything on it."

Bryn nodded and ducked back into the room as Kat and I followed. She kicked off her shoes and flopped onto my bed as I wedged myself in the middle of them both. Kat sniffed delicately and I tried not to laugh.

"Duvet Day," I said by way of explanation and she nodded like she understood—was this just a thing everyone but me had known about?

"Was I just mega drunk last night or did I hear Xander say that you're going to play basketball with him and Ryan this week?"

I groaned. "Don't remind me. Bryn thinks I need a new hobby."

"You might love it," Bryn said as she finished ordering the food on her phone.

Kat and I shared a look before she opened her mouth and agreed with Bryn, the traitor. "I think it'll be good for you."

I rolled my eyes. I wasn't sure how basketball with Jamie's boyfriend was going to solve all my problems but it would at least give me something to do seeing as I still hadn't been to class last week. Though, I had done a virtual taster session via online lecture of a couple of different courses Winters had sent to me—they had been... fine.

"I thought you didn't have any plans today?" Bryn asked as she tipped her head over to re-do her messy bun.

"I didn't," I said honestly, darting a glance at Kat and found her oblivious as she frowned at her phone in her hand, thumbs furiously tapping out a message.

"So what are we watching?" Kat threw her phone down and turned it over so she couldn't see the screen. Something was definitely going on and I would bet money that it had to do with Max and the smear of lipstick I'd seen on his collar last night.

"*The Vampire Diaries*," I told her again. "We're close to finishing season two."

Kat's eyes lit up and she clapped excitedly. "Oh my god, yes! This is such a good season. But, oh, poor Je—"

I clapped a hand over her mouth. "No spoilers!"

Bryn shook her head, lips parting in dismay. "Jeremy?

Jenna? What have you done to me?" She glared at me accusingly and I laughed. She was going to lose it. Not that I could blame her, it was a killer finale.

"No more talking," Bryn warned us, waggling a finger between us before going to grab the food from the delivery guy who'd just knocked at the door.

"What's going on with you two?" Kat looked directly at me, pinning me down as soon as Bryn was out of earshot.

"Nothing except friendship."

"You seem... cozy."

"Can't two women who also happen to like other women be friends?"

Bryn walked back in the room and blinked at my words before wordlessly passing around the pizza.

Kat opened her mouth and shut it quickly when I pinched her arm.

"Ready to have your heart wrecked?" I said cheerfully and Bryn settled in beside me as I hit play.

"Bring it on."

CHAPTER EIGHT

Bryn's place was absolutely fucked.

"How the heck did this even happen? Like, this was a serious flood. Doesn't the landlord have to do checks or something? Maintenance?"

Bryn stood in the doorway to her room, looking somewhat hopeless and I understood why. The carpet was so soggy it had swelled and squelched unpleasantly when we took a step into the room. The stench of mildew and old water was thick in the air, as well as dust where the ceiling had partially fallen in. Unfortunately, her desk had been hit the worst because of its proximity to the hole. Puddles of water still pooled on the cheap surface and the books that had managed to dry out were crispy and stiff—some didn't open at all.

I hesitantly placed a hand on her back. "I'm sorry. It's going to be okay."

She was unnaturally still and I realized she was holding her breath to fight back tears when I saw the glossiness of her gaze. A pat on the back was not going to do the trick here. We'd come to assess the damage now that the water had been shut off and the room had been somewhat aired out, to see if there was anything we could salvage, but the majority of her stuff was wrecked. The clothes she could probably dry clean, but the few nicknacks and photos she had were too waterlogged to save.

I hugged her hard and ran my hand through the ends of her long hair as she shook against my shoulder.

"Sorry, sorry." She breathed deeply and wiped her eyes. "Stupid to cry over stuff."

"No it's not. This was *your* stuff, you have a right to be upset, to be mad, even."

"Honestly the biggest loss is my textbooks, I think I can save a lot of my clothes and my laptop was with me at the time. I didn't really bring much with me when I moved here."

I understood that. I'd traveled pretty lightly when I'd left St Agatha's too. "Bet you wish you'd stayed in Cali now."

"Cali is overrated and overly expensive. Besides," she gave me a watery smile that I returned, "the company here is much better." She pulled out her phone and took a video of the room, as well as a few pictures presumably for evidence.

"Flattered," I said lightly. "You know you can stay with us for as long as you need, so don't worry about that, but I don't think there's much for us to collect here. Why don't we go shopping? Get you some new clothes? You must be running out of stuff."

Bryn shrugged but then her eyes lit up. "This is perfect, actually. If we go to the mall we can check another thing off your list." Ah. The list. I'd almost forgotten... and kind of hoped she had too. No such luck. "Why don't we invite Jamie and Kat as well?"

"Sure," I murmured, digging my cell phone out of my back pocket and shooting a quick message off to them both. "I haven't really told them anything about the list, or you, yet. Kat knows a bit but..."

Bryn shrugged. "That's fine. You don't owe anyone anything, Liv."

I swallowed hard. "I guess."

Bryn walked over to her desk, her shoes sinking into the floor oddly as it bubbled beneath our feet, and picked up a photo that still had a pin sticking out of it where the water had knocked it from the board on her wall.

"Kind of wish this one hadn't been ruined," she said softly, fingers delicate on the edges of the mostly-ruined picture. "I'm not sure I have it in digital."

She put it back on the desk and busied herself on the other side of the room, checking on her small bookshelf to see if there was anything she could potentially dry out properly, and I quickly slipped the photo into my pocket. Bryn wanted me to find new hobbies, and she was helping me so much for nothing in return, so maybe I could find a way to restore this for her. I certainly couldn't make it worse.

Bryn pressed a hand to the wall by the shelf as she stood up from looking at the bottom shelves and then cringed when some of the yellow-beige paint peeled off on her palm. "Let's get out of here before this place falls on top of our heads."

I nodded to myself a little as we left her building, a small bag of stuff all that we could take out of there. Bryn didn't live far from the mall, so we crossed the road and sat on one of the benches in the park as we waited to hear back from Jamie and Kat. "Are you sure you're okay?"

"As okay as I can be." She cleared her throat. "So, we never really had this conversation before, but when I said it's silly to cry over stuff I meant it. Kit and I... Well, we had a lot growing up, but we didn't really have *things*. Our parents prioritized trips and experiences and taught us to value the same."

"Okay?" I was a little confused as to why she was telling me this. A short guy walked past us, a beer in hand and I wrinkled my nose when he leered at us.

"I just mean that there's very few things in my life that aren't replaceable, and even fewer that I'm sentimental about."

Oh. *Oh.* "Bryn, are you trying to tell me that your family is well-off?"

"It's usually better for me to tell people sooner rather than later," she said in a rush of breath. "Otherwise they feel like they've been lied to or something."

"I don't think it's really anyone's business unless you decide that it is," I said firmly and she stared at me. "I mean, thanks for telling me and all. But I'm not exactly a stranger to money."

She laughed and it sounded forced. "Right."

I stopped her with a hand on her arm. "What am I not getting?"

"Nothing."

"Bryn."

"Oh, hey, looks like Jamie texted the group back—"

"*Bryn.*"

"People treat me differently! Once they know," she said more quietly, "they expect different things from me, or they want to be my friend for the things they think I can do for them."

"Okay." I frowned as a passing car revved too loudly for me to speak over. "But like I said—"

"Liv, there's having money and there's having *money*."

"Well, do you mean like the living-comfortably kind? Or the buy-a-small-island kind?"

"The latter," she muttered and I huffed.

"Huh. Well, I guess that explains why you had so much therapy. Rich kids can be dicks." A startled laugh flew out of her and I smiled. "It doesn't matter to me. I guess you're not becoming a lawyer for the money then?"

"No, I'm going to start a not-for-profit firm. Pro bono."

"That's amazing," I said, truly impressed and she waved a dismissive hand in front of her. I checked my messages and saw Bryn had been right. Jamie and Kat had both replied in the group chat to say they'd meet us at the mall. That wasn't the only notification waiting for me though, there was one more.

Missed call. *Dad.* I swallowed past the lump in my throat before dismissing it so it wouldn't show up on my phone again. I wasn't going to lose control this time. My parents didn't get to impact my life and make me feel like this, not any more.

Bryn nodded when I showed her the message from Jamie and we stood to walk up the sidewalk that led to the mall as I did my best to put my dad out of my head.

The mall was slightly further out of town than the bars and restaurants, but still easily walkable and that was one of my favorite things about Sun City. There were still some cars on the road, but most people walked or cycled to get around so it felt generally more peaceful. Bryn's apartment sat between the mall and the football stadium, but it was still noisier near there than where Jamie's was thanks to the main road that led into and out of town.

"So what are you going to get?" Bryn looked at me out of the corner of her eye and I decided to play dumb.

"Oh, you know, bits and pieces..."

"Olivia," she said tauntingly and I sighed.

"I don't know. I haven't thought about it."

"You wrote it," she protested and I pouted.

"Yeah, but it was late at night and I was clearly suffering from late-night-hysteria."

"That's not a thing."

"It could be." I blinked innocently at her and when she continued to stare, I relented. "You guys can pick."

"That's not the point of the list! You're supposed to choose it for yourself."

"Well, then I'll see what I think when I get there."

Bryn squeezed my arm gently. "You've got this. This is supposed to be fun."

I nodded, but internally I was already running through all the stores in the mall, trying to remember exactly what was in there.

Buy something scandalous. That was what I'd put on my list. While I'd definitely broadened my horizons when it came to going out clothes since I'd been at Radclyffe, there were still lots of things I steered clear from—my mother's voice chastising me in my head when I looked too long at a lacey piece of lingerie or a particularly sexy dress. The first vibrator I'd bought had sat unopened in its box for at least a month before I'd felt brave enough to open it without feeling like I was doing something dirty. It was natural, but I'd often been told the opposite growing up, at least through implication if not directly.

The mall loomed up ahead far faster than I'd anticipated, but I relaxed when I saw Jamie and Kat approaching from the direction of the small parking lot—Jamie must have decided to drive. Not a bad decision for one of us to have a car if we ended up buying a lot.

"Hey," I called and we walked in together, the familiar sounds settling my nerves as people chatted in the food court and milled in and out of stores.

"What prompted this trip?" Jamie was watching me carefully, she'd been doing that a lot since I'd walked out of *The Box* a couple of weeks ago. I understood that she was trying to look out for me, but it was spooking me more than helping me.

"Bryn needs more clothes after the flood wrecked a lot of hers." Kat cooed sympathetically and I peered at her when she wasn't looking. "So what's new with you?"

"Me?" Was it my imagination or was she squirming a bit too much to not be hiding something? "Oh, you know. Nothing much. Just work. The usual."

Jamie raised an eyebrow at me and I gave her a tiny nod. So it wasn't just me who had noticed Kat's recent shiftiness.

"I, um, also need to get something." They all peered at me and I grimaced. "Bryn is helping me with a... project. I need to buy myself something scandalous."

Jamie grinned. "Hell *yes*. Oh, I am so down for that."

I tried not to let my thoughts go anywhere inappropriate after that comment, and managed fairly well. "Cool." I cleared my throat and nodded for emphasis.

"So what's the project for? Class?"

"Actually, kind of the opposite," I said slowly. "They want to kick me off the course." I held up a hand to ward off the flood of protests and questions I could already see forming. "It's fine, I hate it anyway. But Bryn is trying to help me figure out what exactly I might enjoy."

"How is buying something scandalous going to help with that?" Kat said dubiously and Bryn grinned in a way that was both a little intimidating and a little scary.

"The things we're scared of say a lot about us," she said easily and I laughed awkwardly before protesting as Jamie dragged us into what looked like a lingerie shop.

"Go wild," she said with a throaty laugh. "Pick out whatever scares you the most."

Why had Bryn thought this was a good idea again?

I looked around the store with begrudging

admiration. It was gorgeous, the space was bright and open with fake florals and plants on the walls and in between the displays. Neon pink light-up signs marked out the different sections of the store and I instantly made a bee-line for the sleep and loungewear section.

"Is this place new?" I muttered as I browsed. "I swear I've never seen this place before."

"I think they opened up a week or so ago." I jumped and turned to find Bryn standing behind me, looking amused as she watched me sulkily sort through silky negligees and cute sleeping eye masks. "Found anything you like yet?"

I held up the pink embroidered eye mask hopefully and Bryn narrowed her eyes.

"Does that scare you?" I shook my head. "Then put it back. Or get it anyway, I don't care, but the objective is to find something you would normally be too nervous to buy."

I sighed. "I know."

The thing that really rankled me was that there were some truly gorgeous things in this store and I'd only been looking for five seconds. I guess part of me had hoped I wouldn't see anything I liked, because surely Bryn wouldn't make me buy something I hated just for the sake of it? Unfortunately, it didn't look like that was going to be a problem.

I brushed my hand across a sheer bodysuit as I walked through the store. It was stunning, a dark green with embroidered butterflies in deep pinks covering the area over the boobs, a little scandalous but not completely out there.

I slowly picked it up and draped it over my arm and glanced over at Bryn like I was a kid who'd been caught doing something naughty, only to find her browsing a nearby rack herself. She held up a two-piece that was barely fabric, just dark red straps criss-crossing in a configuration that was as mind-boggling as I was sure it would be difficult to get on. I swallowed hard as I thought about how fun it would be to unwrap someone wearing that particular piece though, the way it would curl around curves and tease you by being covered and yet bare. Bryn looked up and I blinked, realizing I had been staring, and turned away quickly.

I kept walking until I came across a slightly more sedate display than what Bryn had been checking out, but only slightly. A baby pink piece caught my eye and I lifted it from the rack to examine it better. It was a balconette bra, sans actual cups, garter belt, and sheer pink panties with a lace overlay. It looked a little strange on the bottom though, and when I turned it over I saw why. Crotchless.

I could feel myself blushing, but I didn't put it down. It really was a cute set, and the lack of barriers in the... crotch area, could definitely come in handy.

I hesitated for a second more before adding it to the small pile I was holding in my arms.

"You found something?"

I jumped. "God, I need to put a bell on you." I held up my pick gingerly and Bryn went completely still. "What is it? Is it not daring enough?"

Jamie and Kat walked over and an appreciative look came over Kat's face as she saw what I was holding up. "Ooh, does it come in black?" She rifled through the rack I nodded to and Jamie looked between Bryn and me with some unreadable expression on her face.

"Maybe you should try it on," she suggested, glancing at Bryn again, and I frowned.

"That wasn't part of the deal—"

Bryn had gone pale. "I don't think that will be necessary."

Jamie shrugged, like it didn't matter to her either way, and that didn't sting as much as I'd thought it would.

"What's wrong?" I asked Bryn quietly as we walked toward the checkout.

"Nothing," she said stiffly and I shifted uneasily.

"Okay." What else could I say? If she didn't want to talk to me, I couldn't force her.

I paid for the bodysuit, the pink set, and the sleep mask and then dutifully followed Kat into a bookstore, giving their romance section a cursory glance but leaving empty handed while Kat stacked four books atop each other.

By the time we made it to the small smoothie place in the food court, Bryn seemed fine. She was smiling and joking and had accumulated a couple of bags of her own. We could probably store some of her stuff in Jamie's room until she could move into her new place. The thought made me feel a little sad. I'd grown used to having her around. Though I guessed it would be nice to have the living room back when she left, and it wasn't like we had to stop hanging out just because she wasn't my roommate anymore.

"What are you thinking so hard about?"

"Hm? Oh, just how quiet it'll be when you move out."

"Missing me already, Liv?" The playfulness was back in her expression and I smiled.

"Yeah."

I didn't miss the look Kat and Jamie gave each other at my response, but I couldn't bring myself to care. Let them think what they wanted. I glanced at Bryn and saw her masking her surprise at my words, but it couldn't be that surprising that I liked her company? We hung out all the time, we were friends, and I would miss having my friend in my living room. It was as simple as that really.

"Did you guys drive here?" Better to steer the conversation into safer waters seeing as I still didn't know what had got to Bryn earlier. "You looked like you came from the parking lot when we walked in."

"Oh, no. We just came from the other direction because Ry and some of the guys were playing football."

The sound of his name in her mouth didn't fill me with instant jealousy, so did that mean exposure therapy was working already so soon? "I thought the season was over?"

"It is—it was just a friendly game."

I had no idea what that meant, but I nodded anyway and tried not to laugh when Bryn looked at me with the same cluelessness on her face. "I guess we can all walk back together then?" I turned to Kat, who nodded and smiled.

"Yeah I have a shift at the bar so I'll head back with you guys too."

The crowds had died down a little as we made our way out of the mall and back toward the park to head home. Even though we'd only walked around a few shops I was glad to be leaving. My social battery had started to drain about half an hour ago.

"So that's an item ticked off the list." Bryn swung her bag in her hand as she walked and I nodded. "What should we go for next? Skinny dipping? Driving lessons? Smoke a joint? What was the one about the orga—"

I clamped a hand over her mouth and felt her laugh tickle my fingers.

"Okay, now we *need* to know more about this project —" Jamie started as Kat nodded enthusiastically, but then a loud voice had us all jumping.

"Aw, look up sweetheart. Pretty girl like you should always be smiling."

I stared in confusion at the short guy with the square face who was approaching us from the opposite direction. Was he shouting at us? It looked like the same guy who'd watched Bryn and me so closely earlier when we'd been sitting on the bench, but now he was sans beer can—it was hard to tell though without my glasses on.

"No need to be rude," he called again as he walked closer. "All I want is a smile."

Jamie seemed content to just walk past him and I breathed a sigh of relief, until he screamed at her almost directly in her face.

"Hey, bitch. I said, *smile*."

Fuck.

Jamie froze on the spot and if I didn't know her better, I might have assumed fear had seized her muscles. But I did know her better and it was anger, not fear, that kept her rooted to the ground as she slowly turned her head and offered the man the sweetest, most dazzling, smile that he almost didn't seem to register her words.

"Go fuck yourself, you sack of shit."

I had the feeling this was going to end badly.

Sure enough, the guy's white face reddened as he stepped forward and got into Jamie's space, spittle flying from his mouth as he tried to intimidate her. I could have saved him a lot of time if he'd bothered to ask, because there wasn't a chance in Hell that Jamie was going to back down and that was bad news for all of us.

"Think you're tough, little girl? Stupid bitch. Wouldn't want to fuck you anyway." His hands were balled into fists and with every word he seemed to try and crowd into her space even more.

I reached for Bryn, gripping her hand tightly as I tried to assess the situation. *Should we run? Call the cops?*

Jamie didn't move away, just smiled again but this time with a razor sharp edge as she spat in his face, "Cunt."

He swung and I screamed. It was broad daylight! This shit shouldn't happen at all, but something about the sun shining cheerily overhead made it all feel worse.

His fist never connected. One second he was twisting his body and the next he was on the floor, writhing in pain.

I looked at Jamie, dropping Bryn's hand as I moved to her. "Are you okay?" I grabbed her shoulders and examined her, but she seemed fine, if a little shaken that the guy had leapt at her like that. I checked her hand and blinked when I didn't see a wound.

"Stay down," a sharp voice said and my mouth dropped open when I turned to see Kat pinning him to the ground, a fierce expression on her face that I'd never seen before.

"Kat," I breathed, unsure what to do or how to help. "What do you need?"

"Should we call the cops?" Bryn's face was paler than usual and I moved closer to her, not liking the way her hands were shaking.

"He didn't technically do anything," Kat said reluctantly. "I had him on the ground before he made contact."

"How did you do that?" I didn't think I'd ever admired her more than I did at that moment. She was like a freaking superhero.

The guy on the ground seemed to have passed out from whatever hold Kat had put him in and she nodded to the pathway ahead of us as she let him go. "I've been taking self-defense classes, didn't think I'd really have to put it into practice though."

We left the guy on the ground as we walked quickly away until he was out of sight around a bend in the pathway and then Bryn rounded on Jamie.

"What the fuck is wrong with you?"

I realized somewhat belatedly that the shaking of her

hands had been anger, not fear, as she stepped into Jamie's space and stared her down.

"Me? *I* wasn't the one screaming in our faces, that was the other guy."

Bryn's jaw tightened and, as her fists clenched, I wasn't sure I'd ever seen her so mad. I hesitantly tried to step between them and Bryn pressed a cautionary hand on the front of my shoulder, holding me away. "You put us all at risk with your stupid fucking antics. If Kat hadn't saved your ass we might have all ended up seriously hurt. You might not care about your own safety, but have a little thought for the people around you. Jesus."

Bryn turned away without another word and marched off.

Jamie looked at Kat and me with big eyes. "What was her problem?"

I frowned. Sure, that guy had been out of line, but Jamie had been as well for baiting him. What if he'd had a gun? "Sometimes, I wish you'd think a little more about the situation and other people before you go around pissing people off."

"Liv—"

I held up a hand. "No. I'm sorry, but Bryn was right." I hesitated before stepping forward and gently squeezing Jamie's arm. "Sometimes the safer thing for everyone is just to let things go."

I turned around and followed after Bryn, walking a little faster than before to catch up with her until I was breathless by the time I reached her side. She glanced at me as she walked on, her body tense and her jaw tight.

"Don't fucking defend her, Liv. She deserved that and you know it."

"Are you okay?"

Her mouth was pressed into a flat line and I could see the anger starting to fade, fear replacing it as she walked faster. "I can't believe that happened."

"Me either."

"You could have been hurt."

I blinked, surprised that was her first thought, and then froze when she stopped in her tracks and roughly pulled me to her. Her body was trembling, and I held her back just as tightly as she gripped me. "You could have been hurt."

"I'm alright," I murmured into her hair. "You're okay, we're okay."

Bryn pulled back, breathing out shakily as she continued walking. "I shouldn't have yelled at her."

"You were scared and emotions were running high. She won't blame you."

We slowed our pace to let Jamie and Kat catch up to us and for a second the tension was unbearable until Bryn sighed. "I'm sorry. You did a dumb thing, but that guy was the asshole. Not you."

"No." Jamie shook her head. "I'm sorry. To all of you. I wasn't thinking, I just reacted and I put you all at risk."

"Let's just get home—in one piece," I added as I looked between the two of them. It was not going to be pretty when we told the guys what had happened.

I wrinkled my nose. Maybe I'd leave that to Jamie.

CHAPTER NINE

"I CANNOT BELIEVE THAT BRYN YELLED AT Jamie," Xander said wonderingly as he bounced the ball between his hands expertly. I stood in front of him, shuffling awkwardly from side to side as I attempted to block him from getting past me. Xander stepped and bounced, the ball flying between his outstretched leg as he darted past me and leapt for the hoop. "To be honest, I can't imagine *anyone* having balls big enough to shout at Jamie."

I met his jump, my long arms brushing the bottom of the ball but ultimately missing as it sank in and I cursed. The boys had been less than amused with our story of what had happened after the mall, but things between Bryn and Jamie had been fine if a little overly-nice at home.

"You're doing good," Ryan reassured me as he wiped the sweat off his face, "plus you're tall which is always a bonus in these kinds of ball games."

"I'm not surprised," Kit said with a grin as he glanced at Xander. "Bryn's not one to hold back."

I shrugged. "Honestly Kat was the one that shocked me the most."

Xander caught the ball on its descent and tucked it under an arm as he swigged some water from his bottle and I moved to the side of the outdoor court to do the same. It was ungodly hot out for eleven in the morning and I found myself grateful that we hadn't waited until the afternoon to play, because I might have passed out from heat exhaustion.

"Did Kat really tackle him?"

I jumped, not having heard Leo approach. He somehow looked cool, only a slight tinge of pink in his cheeks as he stretched out his lean muscles and I wondered if maybe I'd been wrong before—maybe he was interested in Kat.

"It was a bit more graceful than a tackle, it was like she triggered a pressure point or something."

Xander whistled and I couldn't help but agree. I never would have thought that Kat was capable of such fierceness, not that she wasn't a badass in her own right but Jamie shone so strongly in that regard it was hard to see anybody else. If anything, Jamie had been... reckless. I wasn't mad at her, but it did worry me how little regard she held for her own safety. If I responded like that to every guy who hollered at me, I would probably have been beat up a million times over, or worse.

I pulled Kit to one side before he could rejoin the guys

starting to resume playing again on the course. "I was wondering if you could help me with something?"

He paused, waiting for me to say more and I held back a smile. He was taking the whole overprotective brother thing to a whole new level with me and Bryn.

"Bryn and I went to check out her place yesterday before the mall and it was a mess, there wasn't much we could do. But there was this photo—"

"I know the one," he said, eyes following Leo as he dove for the ball in Xander's grip. "She mentioned it to me yesterday on the phone."

"Right," I said, clearing my throat. "Well, I took it."

"What? Why?" He was looking at me like I was crazy and I squeezed my hands together tightly.

"I wanted to see if I could restore it for her somehow, to say thanks for everything she's helping me with," I said hastily, not liking the way his eyes were narrowing. I knew what it sounded like and didn't even want to address it. If I ignored the implications, then they wouldn't exist, right? "But I did some research and I don't think it's going to be possible because of the damage. So then I thought, what if I could recreate it?"

Interest flared across Kit's face and I relaxed. He was intrigued, so he would help me, plus it would make Bryn happy. "You want to paint it?"

"Whatever you recommend—I've not done any artwork for a long time but I used to be okay at it."

Kit nodded thoughtfully as he half-watched the game. "If it were me, I would sketch it first and then paint it —watercolors."

"Amazing," I breathed. "Thanks, Kit. Would you, um, want to help?"

He looked at me long and hard before nodding slowly. "Sure, but make sure she understands what this is," he warned as he backed away from me to join in the game. "Or rather, what it's not," he said pointedly and I nodded even as I thought he was being ridiculous. This wasn't a romantic gesture, it was just one friend doing something nice for another friend.

A loud shout had me looking up quickly and I shrieked as I caught the basketball as it hit my face, my head snapping back from the force of the throw.

"Oh shit! Liv! I'm so sorry, are you okay?"

I dropped the ball and Leo rushed over to me, I was pretty sure it was the most emotion I'd ever seen from him.

"Xander tackled me and I accidentally threw it. I didn't mean to hit you."

I swallowed past the slight ringing in my ears and tried to smile. "S'alright."

"You're slurring," Ryan pointed out and I squinted at him.

"You might have a concussion," Leo muttered before wrapping one arm around my shoulders and the other around my legs as he hoisted me up and into his arms.

The ground rolled and I closed my eyes. "What are you doing?" I tried to ask, but it came out more like *whaterndoon* and several faces pressed into the space around mine as they peered at me worriedly.

"I think there's a clinic on campus," one of the

voices said and I decided to just sit back and let them decide what should be done while I relaxed in Leo's arms.

My head was throbbing as we started to move and I couldn't help but find it funny that it was Leo carrying me, of all people. He was nice enough but seemed kind of quiet whenever we got together in a big group—in fact, today had been the most relaxed I'd ever seen him. Until he'd hit me in the face with a basketball.

The nurse clinician gasped when we walked in and I knew I should probably be concerned that I couldn't remember the walk from the courts to campus, but I was only capable of giggling as I imagined the picture we must have made as the whole group of guys crowded into the room.

The nurse looked me over and decided I had whiplash and possibly a light concussion, but that I was okay to go home and take it easy so long as I got medical attention if I felt worse.

Jamie and Bryn were home by the time I got back and they gaped as Ryan carried me through the door to deposit me on the sofa. I wasn't exactly heavy, and the walk from campus to the apartment was probably just over twenty minutes, but the guys had traded off as they walked me back, each taking a turn to carry me. Thankfully, I didn't puke on anyone, so the concussion couldn't have been that bad.

"What did you do to her?" Jamie demanded and Leo sheepishly rubbed the back of his neck.

"Um, the basketball hit her in the face." Both girls

seemed to stiffen in anger until Leo widened his eyes. "By accident! It was an accident."

"Accident," I confirmed with only a little difficulty pronouncing all the letters in the right place.

Bryn bit her lip and looked at me until we both burst out laughing at the same time. I waved her off after a couple of seconds, my head pounding, and Leo continued as Jamie stared at us, baffled.

"So, yeah. She has whiplash. And a concussion," Leo said with a grimace.

"I feel like only you could go out to play basketball and somehow get whiplash and concussed," Bryn said as she rolled her eyes. "I shouldn't laugh, but your luck is just so ridiculous."

"Ridiculous," I repeated with a nod that made me wince as it jarred my head.

"I mean, a *concussion*," Bryn repeated, bemused.

"Light," I corrected, dragging the word out before smiling. "I think basketball's not really for me, Bryn."

"I'll let you off," she murmured as she moved my legs to sit down on the sofa, dropping them back down into her lap. "I'm guessing that means no yoga tomorrow as well?"

"My abs will survive missing one session," I quipped and something sparked in her eyes that had interest shivering through me in return.

"Rest up," she said, rolling her eyes and Jamie shooed the guys out of the flat, pressing a kiss to Ryan's slightly sweaty face as she did so.

"I really am sorry, Liv," Leo called as Jamie herded

them out and I waved a hand airily at him. "If you need anything, let me know."

I thought about it as he left and Bryn watched me, a small smile flirting with her mouth.

"What is it?"

"Do you think I could guilt Leo into bringing me some ice cream?"

She laughed. "I think you could get him to make it from scratch.

I smiled as I closed my eyes, relaxing against the pillows as Bryn covered me with a blanket. "Excellent."

"I did it." I flopped back down into my seat at the booth Bryn and I had chosen at *The Box*, phone clutched triumphantly in my hand. Three days later, and I'd been cleared by the doctor to be up and about again. Aside from a little lingering soreness in my neck, I felt absolutely fine. Bryn had taken my bed for the first night while I crashed on the sofa, but I'd felt okay enough to swap back the next day.

"And she definitely has never sold you drugs?"

"Nope."

Bryn smirked. "Baby girl's growing up. What did you say to her?"

I shrugged. "I just asked if I could have her number."

From the look on Bryn's face, this wasn't quite the

answer she'd hoped for. "So you didn't make small talk? Or introduce yourself?" I shook my head and she sighed. "Well, you may have zero game but at least you did it."

"Gee, thanks." I took a sip of my milkshake, they were definitely my new go-to even if they did give me both brain freeze and a sugar crash afterwards. "How're things with you and Jamie now?"

"Fine." Bryn shrugged. "She was stupid, I was stupid, and now we're good."

"The guys all seemed impressed that you stood up to her."

Bryn rolled her eyes as I sipped my drink. "They make her sound like a pitbull or something."

I snorted and Bryn stood up from the table.

"Anyway, I have to get back to the apartment to study. You coming?"

"Sure." I sucked the last of my milkshake down and then shivered as the cold ran through me. "Wait, what are you studying for?"

"I've got an exam."

"And you're wasting your time with my stupid problems rather than revising?" I slapped her arm lightly as we walked out and into the warm late-afternoon air. "You idiot."

"Helping you," she reminded me dryly and the look I gave her made her sigh. "It's just one exam, everything else I already sat when I was in Cali. I just need to pass this one unit."

"I'm sure you'll be fine."

Bryn waggled her eyebrows. "Want to help me maneuver my flash cards?"

"How can I say no to an offer like that?" She laughed and I grinned. "No, seriously, how do I say no?"

"Can you be bribed?" A sly look came over her face, "because if so, I have a gift for you."

Now I was intrigued. "Maybe."

We walked inside the apartment and I kicked off my trainers before placing them neatly on the rack I'd insisted we buy. I hated it when the hall got cluttered up with shoes, whereas Jamie would probably have never even noticed them there.

I sank into the sofa, nudging Bryn's pillow out of the way, and waited for her as I reached for the flash cards she'd already made and placed on the table.

Bryn plopped down next to me, exchanging her flashcards for the box she held in her hand. She almost looked... nervous.

"I picked this up for you the other day at the mall, it's for item number five on the list."

I immediately blushed. God. Item number five. What had I been thinking? I couldn't believe I'd even written it down, let alone showed another living, breathing person.

"Now, I want you to know that there's no pressure and no expectations. I just thought this might be a good way to tick that box without, um." Now Bryn was the one who was turning pink as I watched in fascination. "...exposing yourself too much."

I finally looked down at the little pink box and stared.

"You don't need to use it with me," Bryn said in a

rush. "I could find you a date, or there might even be a manual mode so you can, ah, operate it yourself. Obviously, I'll help if you'd rather it be a... friend."

My mouth went dry. It was a small, vibrating egg—according to the description on the box anyway. It came with a remote control and—*wow*—seven different settings. I thought back to number five on the list and considered the toy, I guessed it did fit.

5. Have an orgasm in public

I wasn't sure my blush would ever fade at this point. While I'd kissed in public, that was about as far as it had ever gone and I was... curious.

"Thank you," I said finally, realizing I'd probably been silent for far too long. "Um, yeah. This could work."

We looked at each other and burst out laughing. "I'm sorry," she gasped as more giggles snuck free. "I just saw it and thought of you."

I couldn't control the laughter that spilled out of me, tears escaping my eyes as I wheezed for breath. "When should I use it?"

"I do have an idea for that." The gleam in her eye had intrigue raising its head inside me and I nodded for her to continue, but she only smirked. "You'll have to wait and see."

"Fine." I pouted and she rolled her eyes, shuffling through her flash cards while I went to leave the toy in my room. I grabbed a bag of candy from the kitchen on my way back before I sat down again. "Okay, now for *your* bribe. One piece of candy per correct answer."

Bryn had a ridiculous sweet tooth and the way her eyes lit up at the brightly coloured bag in my hands made me feel stupidly smug.

"When did you pick those up?"

I waved off her question. "No more stalling. Ready?"

She sat up straight, her face calm and focused in a way that even centered me.

"Ready."

CHAPTER TEN

"Why are we doing this today? We should be out celebrating your exams being over!" Bryn ignored me, keeping her eyes firmly on the road as I attempted to needle her. "Come on," I whined. "Just tell me where we're going." I gave her my best puppy dog eyes and her lips twitched.

We'd been in Jamie's car for about forty minutes already and I had no clue what Bryn was up to. She'd simply told me we were going out for the day and to pack some lunch which gave me... nothing to go off.

"We're going," she said finally as the car began to slow and she took a turning off the main road and onto what looked like a dirt path, "to kill three birds with one stone."

I furrowed my brows, confused, until we rounded a bend and a gate stood in our way, blocking a dense patch of woods and, just visible through the trees, a glimmer of water. Bryn hopped out and unlocked the gate before driving us back through and locking it again.

Three birds with one stone? What did she—

We drove further into the woods and then I saw the glimmer of water was actually a huge lake, complete with a small dock.

Three birds with one stone.

We were in Jamie's car. By a lake. A *secluded* lake. Either Bryn was about to murder me or...

Driving lessons. Weed. Skinny dipping.

My head snapped quickly towards Bryn and she laughed when she caught the expression on my face.

"Yep," she said smugly. "Kind of perfect, right? Just tell me you know how to swim."

I stared at her. "Of course I do."

She shrugged. "Hey, I'm not judging. Some people don't."

I didn't say anything else, nerves beginning to settle in. Bryn was going to see me naked. I mean, yes, she'd technically already seen it that night I'd been drunk after *Luscious*, but this was different. I was sober. It was day time.

Then another, possibly more concerning, thought hit me: *I was going to see* Bryn *naked.* Unless she wasn't planning on coming in with me. Surely she wasn't just going to watch me strip off and swim around though, right?

"So what do you think?" Bryn asked as she pulled the car to a stop not too far from the mini pier. "Do you want to smoke before or after?"

"After," I said immediately. As much as I wanted to not be sober when I got naked, I disliked the thought of swimming while high more. "Does Jamie know you're planning on raiding her car stash?"

"Know?" Bryn snorted. "She insisted on rolling three fresh joints, all in different flavors or something for you to try."

"*Three?* How stoned does she think I'm going to get?"

Bryn grinned. "I think she just wanted to join in somehow."

"And yet you didn't invite her."

She shrugged. "I thought it would be counterproductive to bring you to a secluded spot with the girl you love, but can't have, while she's naked. I didn't take you as a glutton for punishment."

Okay. Point. I inclined my head slightly and Bryn smirked before pushing open her car door and climbing out. Great. I guess we were doing this then.

"Are you, ah, coming in with me?" I stared out at the lake apprehensively. It was a great day to do this, weather-wise, but I hadn't had the time to psych myself up (or out) about it first. I tried to focus on the physical sensations, blocking out the threads of nervousness that threatened to overwhelm me as I inhaled the scent of water and warm grass, the buzz of insects nearby replacing the sound of my heartbeat in my ears.

I could feel Bryn staring at me and I met her eyes before we walked to the edge of the grass.

"Unless you don't want me to?"

"Oh, no, it's fine, I just meant—"

She swept her tee off over head before I could finish speaking and I choked on my own spit at the sight of her breasts pressing against the pale blue bra she was wearing. I froze and she raised an eyebrow.

"You know, to skinny dip you have to take off your clothes."

I nodded jerkily as I kicked off my sandals and reached for the hem of my cotton shorts, stepping out of them clumsily as Bryn tugged down the tight skirt she'd had on and then paused as she waited for me to slip off my top before she unhooked her bra. I tried not to look. Then I tried to be professional, clinical. They were just boobs. Nothing I hadn't seen before and nothing I didn't also own.

But they were *Bryn's*. Her skin was perfectly creamy and slightly flushed with pink, like she was blushing. Her skin was a little tanned, but her breasts were paler than her chest, the tips of her nipples a flushed peach that made me unexpectedly greedy. For what, I wasn't sure.

"Are you going to ogle me? Or get naked?"

I undid my own bra, letting it drop to the ground on top of the rest of my clothes, and shivered as a light breeze touched my skin. It felt strange, to be standing like this out in the open, where anyone could see.

Bryn looked down my body to my underwear, just plain cotton, and there was an intensity to her gaze that hadn't been there a second ago as she said, "You first," and I obeyed.

I turned away before she could drop her own briefs, not trusting myself to look away if I saw all of her, and I'd embarrassed myself enough when it came to her. The wood on the pier was warm under my feet as I walked and

I could feel the gentle vibrations of Bryn's steps as she followed me, but I focused on the sunshine I could feel beating down on me, the sound of the water as it moved with the breeze.

I stopped at the edge and looked down. It was surprisingly clear, sparkling in the sunshine and I could see the bottom so I wasn't too worried about how deep it might be. Bryn came up next to me and the warmth from her arm next to mine had me wanting to lean a little closer.

"So do we just jump?" I asked, not recognizing the breathy quality of my own voice.

"Unless you want to be pushed," she teased and I reached for her hand.

"Together?"

Her fingers closed around mine and squeezed, so I took that as a yes as I bent my legs and we leapt into the water.

I lost my grip on Bryn but found her treading water next to me when I surfaced, water droplets caught in her eyelashes and her hair slicked back from her face, darkened by the moisture.

I shivered a little and swam in a lazy circle to keep warm. The water felt good after being in the hot car for so long and with the sun overhead, we wouldn't get cold any time soon.

"Thank you for doing this," I said quietly to her as we floated on our backs next to each other, hands intertwined once more.

"Felt good, huh."

"Yeah."

I could hear the smile in her voice when she replied. "I'm glad."

Something brushed my leg and I jumped, losing my balance and dipping under the water until I resurfaced, coughing and spluttering, in Bryn's arms. Her skin was slippery but warm as she held me.

"Relax! It was just my foot."

I laughed and suddenly I couldn't stop. Bryn joined in, and with us standing so close together it felt like all I could see was her smile. Her eyes sparkled, a few shades lighter than the water we stood in, her arms keeping me pressed to her chest and sliding up and down my arms as I began to shiver.

"Are you cold?" Her voice was low, husky, and my eyes dropped to her lips and didn't move as I shook my head.

"No," I murmured and our heads tilted.

"Me either," she whispered and then her lips were on mine, tasting and devouring, warmth infusing me from every spot our skin touched. It was a slow exploration, a parting of mouths and a teasing tangle of tongues as I took in every touch, every sound that passed her lips.

She pulled away first and I let her.

"Sorry," she said at last, slightly breathless as she dipped under the water and came back up again. "I don't know what I was thinking."

I didn't know what to say, so I said the only thing I could. "It's alright."

She nodded slightly and I looked away as she pulled herself up and onto the pier where she'd left us a couple of towels each. As I watched her walk away, I had to hope that I hadn't just ruined another good thing in my life.

I followed her out of the water, grabbing the towel she'd left behind, and sat down a decent distance away from her under a tree in the shade. She'd brought the food and drinks out of the car and laid them out on top of another towel and I reached greedily for the grapes at the same time as her, our fingers brushing before I pulled back and studiously stared out at the water.

There was probably only one thing that would help make this less awkward.

I went back to the car and rummaged in Jamie's glove compartment until I found her stash. "Okay, I have no idea which flavor is what, but I doubt we could tell the difference anyway."

I lit the end like I'd watched Jamie do a hundred times, with the joint in my mouth to encourage the flame as I burnt off the end of the paper.

"Now what am I doing with this?"

Bryn smiled but it didn't quite reach her eyes. "Inhale into your mouth, hold and then inhale again, then exhale. Start small," she warned and I nodded as I followed her instructions, re-lighting the joint and promptly coughing as I tried to inhale. Eyes watering, I looked to Bryn who nodded encouragingly. "Go slow. There's no rush. You'll cough a lot at first."

"Do you smoke much?" I would be surprised if the answer was yes, I'd been living with her for a while now and never seen her smoking.

"No, I just asked Jamie what to do because I knew you'd have questions."

That was... very sweet, actually.

I tried another drag, smaller this time and only coughed a little as I offered it to Bryn. She took it from my hand awkwardly, pinching the end as she inhaled and then coughed so hard that I quickly handed her a drink.

We passed it back and forth until I started to feel a little funny and waved her off when she tried to pass it back.

"I think I need a break," I said and then giggled.

Bryn giggled too. "Do you think we could catch a fish in the lake?"

"Maybe, but I don't think we could cook it," I said thoughtfully and then laughed harder when Bryn presented one of Jamie's lighters like it was the solution to that particular problem.

"It would take forever to cook." I pressed my tongue to the roof of my mouth and cringed. "Does your mouth feel like... blurgh?" I said, trying to articulate the feeling and Bryn nodded solemnly.

"It really, really does."

We giggled again and I hadn't even realized I'd been snacking on the grapes again until I put my hand in the box and found it empty.

I didn't remember the time passing until suddenly the sun was slinking a little lower in the sky and we had been laid on the ground for a long while, hair stiff and sticking up in all directions after it had dried in the sun.

"How did you know about this place anyway?"

"I just looked it up."

"What did you search? 'Prime spots for skinny dipping'?"

Bryn chuckled and I was glad that the tension had faded alongside our high. "I just looked for private lakes and then rented it."

I shook my head. "You didn't need to do that. I can pay you back."

She smiled and shrugged. "You and Jamie can consider it payback for letting me crash with you."

"Have there been any updates on your new place yet?"

"They think it'll be ready soon."

Soon. The word seemed to hang between us. Soon, she would be leaving and everything would change again.

"We'll have to take it in turns to host TVD viewing sessions," I said lightly and her instant smile was so bright all I could do was stare.

"I'm sure we can work something out."

I smiled. "Are you sober enough to drive home?"

"Yeah, I'm fine now. But first, I think I promised you a driving lesson."

I looked at Jamie's beat-up car with no shortage of trepidation. "Are you sure that's a good idea?"

She grinned at me. "I can handle you, Liv, don't worry."

CHAPTER ELEVEN

THINGS BETWEEN BRYN AND I WERE FINE. THERE were only two unspoken rules, we didn't speak about her moving out and... we didn't talk about The Kiss.

Sure, we'd kissed before, but not like that. Not like it was everything, like *she* was everything.

So we ignored it.

We'd gotten so good at ignoring it, that when Bryn told me she'd set me up on a date with someone, I could almost pretend I wasn't hurt.

"You winced, did I press down too hard?"

"What?" I blinked up at her as her warm hands slid further down my calf as she pressed it toward my chest. "No. It's fine." It was *not* fine—she'd kissed me, and then set me up on a date after? If that wasn't confusing, then I didn't know what was.

Bryn's hands trailed a path of fire down my legs as she pushed against me and I clenched my hands on the edges of the mat, relieved when the instructor called for us to move on. Except, it didn't get better. Sure, I no longer had to directly run my hands over her body or vice versa, but now I had to watch her back arch as she stretched, or try and avoid staring at the curve of her ass as she bent with her legs straight into a downward dog.

I tried to focus on my breathing, on picturing each move before I did it just like the instructor said, but all I could think about was *her* and all the positions I could get her into. Why did we both have to be so damn flexible?

By the time the class finished, I felt more wound up than when it had started. Bryn wouldn't tell me anything about this date other than where I was meeting her, another thing I was less than happy about—and Bryn seemed to know it, because she steered clear of me for the rest of the day.

I'd got dressed up for the date in the evening, mostly because I wanted to feel good rather than to impress some rando. I wasn't sure what was going on between me and Bryn but I was pretty sure I wanted to be more than friends. I just didn't know where that left me with Jamie. Could I still love her and want someone else? Or had I never really loved her in the first place?

I wasn't sure that they were questions I could answer right then. Instead, I put on the sheer green bodysuit I'd bought at the mall not so long ago with some black skinny jeans and chunky heels, did my make-up to smokey perfection, and felt a smug sort of irritation as Bryn watched me all the way out of the door.

She wanted to set me up on a date? Fine. Then she

could see what she was missing as I walked my ass out the door.

I got to the restaurant a little earlier than my date and couldn't help my surprise when the redhead from *Luscious* sat down opposite me. She was stunning, for sure, but... her eyes had a little too much green mixed in with the blue and I couldn't help wondering what she might have looked like as a blonde.

"So Leah, what do you like to do for fun? Besides party at *Luscious*?"

She smiled and it was dainty and pretty as she dabbed at her mouth with a napkin to clean up non-existent pizza sauce. "Oh, I love to swim."

"I went swimming recently actually, at this little private lake just outside of town..." I cleared my throat as I pictured Bryn, standing in the sun in her baby blue bra and her long hair blowing in the wind.

Leah nodded, eyes bright as she waited for me to continue but instead I bit into my pizza. "That's nice."

Awkward silence descended and it felt like I swallowed too loudly as I reached for my water. "Um, but I actually tried basketball recently."

"I've never played! Did you like it?"

"Yeah, it was great until... Well I actually got a concussion from being hit with the ball."

"Oh."

Crap. Bryn had been right—I had no game.

"But anyway," I said with a smile. "You were telling me about yourself?"

"Right! I love to swim, shop, and I like to take

photographs sometimes too. All normal stuff." Her laugh was tinkling and sweet but I found myself craving something huskier, warmer.

"Oh yeah, I mean, I personally like to hang out in cemeteries writing in my diary." I laughed but it faded awkwardly when she didn't join in. "You know, *The Vampire Diaries*?"

"Sorry, I've never seen it. I only really like non-fiction."

I forced a smile as I nodded. Only liked non-fiction? This was not the vibe for me. Not having seen TVD I could excuse, but the combination of that and the way she'd said *non-fiction,* like it somehow made her better than me, gave me the ick and I was glad when we finished eating and parted ways outside of the restaurant.

She was perfectly nice, polite, and enjoyed a veggie pizza just as much as me, and yet I didn't feel a single tingle when she kissed me goodnight. I didn't discreetly look at her ass when she walked away except to admire the material of the dress she was wearing. Girl had good taste, I had to give her that.

I stepped in through the door to the apartment feeling slightly deflated. Yes, I'd gone on a date and hadn't thought about Jamie once. The only problem was the blonde currently living with us that had taken up residence in my head space instead.

I walked into the living room, intent on giving her one more glimpse of my outfit before I took my heels off, and froze.

"Dad?"

There was no way that my father, who hadn't spoken to me in *months,* was now standing in my living room with Bryn and Jamie. My eyes were so wide with disbelief that I wasn't sure they'd ever go back to their normal size as my dad took in my outfit with a twitch of his eyebrow. It was probably the most daring thing he'd ever seen me wear and I instinctively wanted to cover up even as I straightened my shoulders and met his stare.

"Olivia," he said evenly, hands in the pockets of his blue jeans as he watched me. I took in the vibe of the rest of the room, surprised to see Jamie there but unsurprised to see the defensive stance she'd taken up when I'd walked into the room.

"I told him to leave," she said, half-apology and half-question. I nodded slightly, appreciating the fact that she'd tried to look out for me. "If you don't want him here, I'll make him go."

My dad looked at her thoughtfully, nodding slightly as he turned back to me. "You have good friends."

"I do." I was proud of how steady my voice managed to be in that moment. "What are you doing here?"

"You didn't return my calls."

I fought to keep the surprise off of my face as I thought back to the first notification that had sent me into a meltdown a few weeks ago. "I assumed it was a misdial."

He winced slightly, brown eyes the same shade as mine managing to look wounded at my words and that pissed me off. He had no right to be upset that was what I'd thought when he'd called. They'd been pretty clear that they wanted nothing to do with me. "I want to talk."

I folded my arms across my chest, my heart aching as I looked at his familiar form. He had a few more lines on his face, like he'd aged several years in the past few months, and his salt and pepper beard was now more gray than black but it looked surprisingly handsome against the umber of his skin.

"Where's Mom?"

"She's at home."

Home. As if that was still a word I could associate with the place that they lived, the house I'd grown up in. The silence grew thick between us with all the words I held back and everything he didn't need to say until Jamie stepped between us.

"I think it's best you go." Her voice was sharp and right up until she'd said that, I would have agreed.

"No," I said instead. "Let's talk."

Jamie nodded, her dark eyes worried as they assessed my face. "Okay. We'll be outside if you need us."

I smiled slightly and pressed a quick kiss to her cheek as she left, shutting her bedroom door softly behind her. Bryn didn't look at me as she walked past but I caught her hand before she could leave.

"Will you stay?" I murmured quietly and her eyes flashed to mine, surprised. "Please."

"Of course," she said gently and I breathed a little better when she stayed by my side.

My dad watched us keenly, his eyes falling to the place where I still gripped Bryn's hand. I held it tighter. I wasn't going to compromise who I was for him. Not for anyone.

I only dropped Bryn's hand when I moved to the sofa and gestured for him to sit, too.

"So, talk."

"How have things been, Olivia?"

"Fine." Was he seriously going to attempt small talk? "Tell me why you're here."

He sighed heavily. "I have a friend on the board. When we left... When you enrolled," he corrected, as if not ready to voice the ugly truth: that when they'd *abandoned* me here was the more accurate descriptor. "I asked them to keep an eye on you. They said you might be kicked off your course?"

That was the reason he'd come all the way down here? I'd been avoiding making a decision about my course, but seeing as he was making his disapproval clear... "I no longer wish to continue my studies."

Bryn watched the two of us silently, only intervening to squeeze my hand once as we became more and more formal the longer we talked.

"What I do or don't decide to do with my life is no longer your concern. You saw to that."

"Olivia, you will always be my concern—"

"No," I said, standing up sharply. "You don't get to toss me aside and then pick me up again when it suits you to control my life."

His eyes were wide and his lips bloodless from how tightly he pressed them together. "You're right."

"I—what?"

"I didn't just come here because of Radclyffe. I just... wanted to see you."

"Why?" I couldn't help but ask, voice hushed.

"Because you're my daughter, damn it. Things went too far."

I didn't know what to say, except—"What about Mom?"

He shrugged like it didn't particularly matter. "She agrees."

But she wasn't here. So in other words, she still hated that I was a lesbian and couldn't see past that to the fact that I was her daughter. "I don't want to be somewhere I'm not welcome."

"You are always welcome," he said sternly. "Please, I know I probably don't deserve a second chance. But let me try to fix this. Come to dinner next weekend."

"Dinner?" There wasn't a pie good enough in this whole world to make me forget what had happened or the way they'd stifled me my whole life. Bryn shot me a look and I looked at her incredulously. She thought I should go. "Fine. But only if I can bring Bryn." If she was going to make me do this, then she might as well suffer too.

"Done," my dad said quickly before standing and kissing my cheek while I stood there stiffly. "We'll see you then."

I stayed where I was as Bryn showed him to the door and was still standing in the same place when she came back.

"He's gone."

I nodded, feeling absolutely wrung out. I heard Jamie's door opening and decided I'd people-d enough for one night. For now, I just needed to go to sleep and process this.

"Liv—" Jamie called as I walked past and I smiled tiredly at her as I closed my bedroom door.

"Night."

The light was burning my eyes and I groaned as I rolled over. "Why?"

My bed dipped slightly as a new weight settled on the edge and Bryn's delicate perfume wafted over to me.

"Because it's two in the afternoon and I haven't seen you come out of this room since your dad left."

"So?"

"*So* I don't want you in here wallowing. Not over them."

I sighed as I lowered the duvet from its place above my head to squint at her. The problem was, she was right. Annoyingly. I shouldn't be giving them this power over me, to walk into my life and make me feel... *lesser* like this. Again.

I took a deep breath in and blew it out slowly, repeated it before I opened my eyes to look at her.

She'd opened the blinds in my room and the sunlight streaming in made her blonde hair glow, looking even lighter against the deep purple of the walls Jamie had told me I could paint however I wanted.

"You're a real pain in the ass," I grumbled to her as I swung my legs out of bed and stretched my arms up until they gave satisfying *pops*.

"You're so welcome," she said with a snort before grabbing my hand and dragging me from the room. "Eat. Then we're going out."

"What? No. I really just—"

"Not in charge," she sing-songed and I gritted my teeth.

"Fine."

I ignored the smug expression on her face as I grabbed a poptart from the cupboard and ate it cold as Bryn watched, nose wrinkled. I downed a glass of water for good measure and then raised my eyebrows.

"Happy?"

"Very." Bryn smirked and followed closely behind me as I made my way back to my room. "Don't worry about showering or anything, just grab something comfy and then we're leaving."

My irritation levels were rising alarmingly quickly. Sure, some of that was probably misplaced anger that my dad had just shown up here and expected me to welcome him with open arms or something, but the rest of it felt that Bryn was a busybody who needed to keep her nose out of my life.

...Except for the fact that I'd begged her to do the exact opposite.

I stayed quiet as I tugged on some sweats and pulled my hair up into a high pony. Bryn matched my silence beat for beat and the longer it stretched on, the better I felt. Yeah, she was dragging me out of the house, but she wasn't going to force me to talk about everything that had happened yesterday if I didn't want to and, begrudgingly, I was grateful for that—and for the escape from my thoughts she was providing me with. I'd stayed up late, pacing around my room as I replayed every word my dad had said and everything I hadn't. I'd stood up for myself more than I ever had before, so why didn't that feel like enough?

I reached for my cute, white sneakers as I left my room and Bryn shook her head.

"Those are new, right? Wear something you don't mind getting messy."

That made me pause. Where the hell was she taking me?

I reached slowly for my beat-up gym shoes and laced them on quickly as Bryn made for the door. She led us downstairs and along the edges of the park—the opposite direction of campus. Relief washed through me. I'd been half-worried that she'd signed us up for some on-campus sports or art class.

I let her lead the way as we walked past the long row of bars and restaurants, including *The Box*, before I realized we were walking toward the mall.

"I'm not really in the mood to shop."

"Okay."

I kept my eyes on her face as she continued walking and then rolled my eyes when she offered nothing more than that. "Great," I muttered and saw her lips twitch.

The sidewalk curved away and I stepped automatically

onto the side that would lead to the mall's entrance and hesitated when Bryn walked past. Instead she headed in the direction of a small strip mall on the other side of the parking lot and I squinted to try and read the writing on the building, my eyebrows rising as we finally got close enough for my eyes to make it out.

Sun City Shelter.

I opened my mouth and shut it again as Bryn confidently strolled inside through the automatic door and smiled at the woman behind the counter. Her eyes crinkled at the corners when she smiled back and her gray hair was short and thick, with streaks of white running through it intermittently.

"May." Bryn held out her hand and smiled as the older woman took it. "Thanks so much for having us. This is Olivia."

I smiled and half-waved awkwardly. What on earth were we doing here?

"Of course, I'm always happy to have helpers—especially ones that give us such handsome donations."

Bryn blushed a little and I could tell she was deliberately not meeting my eyes as May led us past a small barrier attached to the painted green-wood desk.

"I figured we'd start small for you before we got to the big boys."

I shot Bryn an alarmed look, no idea what was happening until we walked through a heavy door and the sounds hit me. *Shelter.* As in, *animal shelter.*

My eyes flew wide and I forgot my earlier grouchiness

as excitement built inside me. I'd never had a pet, but I'd always loved animals.

"This here is Marshmallow, she looks grouchy but she's a sweetheart really—aren't you?" May cooed as the orange and white striped cat bumped its head against her hand. The place looked nothing like I was expecting. When I thought of shelters, I imagined long corridors and cages. This was the opposite of that.

We'd walked into a warm room, cozy even, decorated in a sweet tangerine paint with pictures of kittens and cats with what I assumed was their new owners on the walls. The cats milled about, some stretching idly and others playing with toys or snoozing on cat beds or inside cardboard boxes. Several immediately twined themselves between my legs and I let them sniff my fingers before scratching beneath their chin. *So soft.*

I swallowed past the lump in my throat as May pointed out the different cats before leading us over to a cordoned off area with high walls where three kittens snoozed.

"We keep them separate until they get used to the others, otherwise it can get a little overwhelming for them."

I nodded as May bent down and lifted an impossibly small bundle of gray fluff up and out of the pen before handing them to me.

"She doesn't have a name yet," she said as I blinked back tears, the kitten purring happily as she curled up in the crook of my arm. "Somebody dropped her in this morning, found her dumped in the park."

My head snapped up and May nodded at the look on my face.

"Yeah, we get a lot of them just abandoned there. Thankfully the passerby found her quickly, so she hadn't been out there long, and she seems fine."

I passed the kitten back reluctantly after stroking the top of her soft, fuzzy nose.

"Onward then?" May looked to Bryn who gestured for her to lead the way.

I glanced back and felt my heart melt as I saw the tiny kitten with her paws up on the clear perspex of the pen, watching us leave. Ugh, why had Bryn brought me here? It was like she was daring me to bring a little kitten or puppy home.

The next door led to a small corridor that echoed as we walked, the walls a light gray that looked well-maintained. Clearly this place was doing well for itself when it came to donations, and I could see why—the animals were cared for like they were May's own pets.

The sound of barking reached me even before we opened the next heavy door and I couldn't help but be impressed by the system. Even if one of the animals did escape their room, it didn't look like they would be able to leave the facility itself with any ease.

"Our last puppy actually went to its new home yesterday, so it's actually just adult dogs in here right now." We walked through the door and I couldn't help my laugh when a huge golden retriever bounded towards us and placed its paws on my stomach, panting excitedly.

"Hello sweetheart," I crooned as I pet him, a softer

smile landing on my face when I saw Bryn being treated similarly by a fluffy german shepherd.

May strode over to the corner of the room to comfort a more timid looking dog whose breed I couldn't recognise. They were small with a brown and gold coat and big brown eyes, he sniffed cautiously at us before giving a wiggle in May's arms and jumping down to sniff more at my legs and then Bryn's.

"This is Truffle. He's a bit of a scaredy cat with new people."

I sat on the beige laminate floor and waited for Truffle to come over to me, letting him sniff and lick my hand before I stroked over his head and back. Within moments he'd flopped over for belly rubs and May smiled.

"Looks like he likes you."

I hardly even registered her words as the german shepherd made its way over to me too, looking for attention and I smiled at the name on his collar.

"Hey Angus," I murmured as I ran my fingers under his chin, sinking them into his soft fur. His ears hadn't been cropped and folded over each other adorably, as he whined for more pets. "Thank you," I said to Bryn as May distracted the majority of the dogs by putting some food out for them. Only Truffle stayed with me, half on my lap as I stroked him. "This was exactly what I needed."

She sat down next to me and Truffle immediately licked her hand when she reached between us to tickle his belly. "You seem at ease here."

I nodded. It was true. Something about being around animals just made me feel calmer, like all my tension had drained away and any irritating thoughts buzzing around in my brain were finally muffled.

"May was telling me that the girl she was training here moved to Boston recently."

I hummed to show I was listening as I gave my attention to Truffle.

"So she has an opening."

My hand stilled and Truffle gave a tiny bark that made my hand immediately start to move again. "An opening?"

Bryn shrugged. "I mean, if it's not your thing then that's alright, but May needs help running this place and is open to taking on someone new. Even someone inexperienced."

Was she saying...? "Me?"

"It could be," she said, tilting her head to look at the dogs happily munching away on some dried biscuits and letting me process her words before she turned back, her blue eyes burning into mine. "It's up to you."

Me. My choice. *Mine.*

I cleared my throat as I nodded slightly. "What about college?" It was only a small thought at the back of my mind, but this just didn't feel... real. I knew I didn't like my course, knew that academia wasn't the place I wanted to be, but I still somehow felt like I had to do it.

Why? A small voice whispered in my head and the truth was that I didn't have an answer—I'd just spent so long being told that this was the path I had to take that the thought of doing something else almost seemed illogical, even if this would make me happy.

"What about it?" Bryn said with a light shrug and I

wanted to cry, unexpectedly. Maybe the rest didn't need to matter, didn't even bear thinking about. Maybe I just had to do this because it was what felt right, felt *good* even.

I didn't reply, just continued patting Truffle until he finally seemed to realize he was missing out on food and scrambled up to find the bowl waiting for him before one of the other dogs could eat his portion.

May strolled back over to us, her brown-green eyes watching my face intently before she nodded, as if pleased by what she found there. "How're we doing over here?"

"Bryn said you're looking to take on someone new? To train?" I said quickly and May smiled.

"I am."

I swallowed and tried not to grimace, my mouth felt too dry. "I don't have any experience, but I'd be willing to learn if you'd have me."

A pleased smile took over her face as May clasped her hands together in front of her body. "I think I'd like that. These guys seem to like you, and it's clear you like them—there's no better test or qualification than that."

Relief had my shoulders relaxing. "What would the hours be?"

May laughed. "Well, why doesn't Bryn stay here with this lot while you and I go to the front desk to talk more?"

"I'd love that," I said, a little breathless and saw Bryn smile out of the corner of my eye as May turned toward the door. "I knew letting you be in charge of my life was a good idea," I muttered to Bryn as I walked past and she smirked.

"I'll remind you that you said that the next time you're mad I'm dragging you out of bed."

I rolled my eyes but didn't hide my smile as I left her there with the dogs and followed May back to the desk we'd seen on our way in. A strange feeling filled me as we settled into a couple of spinny office chairs and I felt dizzy as I recognized it for what it was: hope.

CHAPTER TWELVE

JAMIE WAS STARING AT ME. SHE'D BEEN shooting me worried glances all afternoon and I was starting to get sick of it.

"I'm fine," I said for what felt like the millionth time.

"If my mom randomly turned up here, I would not be fine."

"Well, my mom didn't," I pointed out and she rolled her eyes. "Look, it's fine. I appreciate your concern. It's just dinner."

"And why is Bryn going with you again?"

What was with the tone? "Moral support."

"Right." Jamie snorted. "Tell me, is she as good as you'd think she'd be? At the 'moral support'?"

"You do realize I'm not sleeping with her."

"Oh, I get it."

"What?" I huffed and Jamie laughed at the grumpy expression on my face as I paused *Pretty Little Liars* again.

"You're in denial."

"Bryn and I are just friends."

"Friends who kiss?"

I threw a pillow at her head. "I told you that because I was confused! Not to use as ammo."

"Confused because you *lo-ove* her."

I slurped my smoothie and ignored her jibing. "Grow up." She opened her mouth again and I shushed her as I hit play. "No. You do not speak during the infamous Haleb shower scene."

Jamie's eyes immediately latched on to the TV and she sighed happily. "Why does this scene just hit different? I would do them both."

I snickered. "Even I can appreciate Caleb superiority."

"Agreed."

"You know, I got Bryn hooked on *The Vampire Diaries*. We're almost at season five now and..." I chattered on and only looked up when Jamie had been suspiciously silent for a long time. "What?" I asked, finding her eyes on me and a soft look on her face.

"Nothing, it's just nice listening to you talk about her."

I sniffed in irritation but could feel my cheeks getting hot. "Whatever," I muttered and Jamie laughed as she stood up to go to the bathroom.

I squinted up at the TV. It was nice having it out of the way on the wall mount, but it was now slightly too high for me to comfortably watch, I'd clearly gotten used to giving my eyes a break when Bryn and I watched on my laptop in bed. I sighed reluctantly before reaching behind the sofa and grabbing a small box discreetly placed on the window ledge.

Just for a few minutes, I thought as I slipped the glasses on. I didn't wear them as much as I was supposed to, but they just got in the way and felt stupid on my face. I couldn't deny the instant relief they brought though. The screen focused and the headache that had been slowly building at the back of my head started to ease.

Then Jamie walked in and saw me. For a second she just stared and then her mouth fell open.

"Since when do you have *glasses?* They look so fucking good. Why don't you wear them all the time?"

I whipped them off my face and glared at her. "You saw nothing."

"Liv, seriously. They're so cute."

I reluctantly put them back on as my eyes began to ache. "Shut up."

She mimed zipping her lips shut and I bit my lip against the smile that tried to break free at her dorkiness. "So what do you think's going on with Kat?" she asked as I took another big gulp of my banana and strawberry smoothie.

"She's definitely being weird, right," I agreed. "Have you seen her with Max at all?"

"Max? No. Why?"

"They turned up to your party at the same time the other week and he had lipstick on his collar that looked like it matched Kat's lips."

"You're like a regular *Sherlock Holmes.*" Jamie grabbed the pillow next to her and clutched it to her chest as she half-watched PLL. "Why would she hide that they were seeing each other though?"

I shrugged. "Who knows what goes on in Kat's brain."

"True." She crunched casually on one of the carrot sticks I'd left out and grimaced. "Where are the real snacks?"

"We're all out."

"Ugh, you and Bryn have decimated my stash."

Of course, that made me think about Jamie's other kind of stash in her car, which made me think about the lake, which made me think about the kiss, which made me think about Bryn, which—

I sighed heavily. "What am I supposed to do about Bryn?"

"Well, for one thing you can ask her to bring some snacks home on her way back from dinner with her mom."

I rolled my eyes. "Not quite what I meant."

Jamie smiled. "I know, babe. You guys will work it out, just take it slow. Let what happens, happen."

"You give the worst advice."

She threw a carrot covered in hummus at me and I dove to catch it in my mouth, crunching happily while she watched in amazement.

"Do your parents know that Bryn's also gay?" I blinked at her, confused as to the segue and she shrugged. "I was just thinking about this dinner, you guys are staying there for the night, right?"

"Yeah."

"And what will the sleeping arrangements be?"

"What are you, my mother? Are you going to ask Bryn her intentions towards me next?" I rolled my eyes but my brain was already running down the possible scenarios. "Why did you give me something else to stress about?"

"Sorry." And to be fair, she did look apologetic.

A key rattled in the door and I quickly packed my glasses away before Bryn could come into the room. Jamie shook her head at me and I pointed at her threateningly as I turned my scowl into a smile when Bryn walked in.

"What're we watching?" she asked as she sank down onto the cushion between Jamie and me and then grabbed a carrot stick.

"*Pretty Little Liars,*" Jamie said when I remained silent. "Have you seen it?"

"Are you kidding me? I'm trash for Shay Mitchell."

They instantly started a game of *fuck, marry, kill* and when Bryn caught my eye and offered me a soft smile, I knew that Jamie was right and I was in trouble.

"Thanks again for this," I said quietly as Kit sketched idly next to me as I attempted to recreate what he'd shown me so far on a piece of practice paper. Obviously I wasn't going to be able to draw anything nearly as good as the photo had likely originally looked, but I could do an approximation with Kit's help—I didn't even know what the photo was supposed to look like. In the end, Kit had drawn the photo as best as he could from memory and now I was working on copying it before I tried experimenting with the paints.

"Of course, it's a nice thought."

I nodded as I sketched a melting ice-cream into younger-Kit's hand. "Yeah, well, Bryn's nice and nice people deserve good things."

"Couldn't agree more," he said, but the words were clipped in spite of his calm expression.

I dropped the pencil and sighed as I turned to him. "What?"

"You kissed her."

God damn it, Bryn. Why did she have to tell her brother everything? "*We* kissed. I didn't kiss her, or it–I —" I frowned. "It's none of your business."

His head jerked up as a muscle in his jaw ticked. "None of my business? I'm her brother."

"And I'm her—Liv," I said awkwardly before turning back to the drawing. It looked awful, Bryn's head was completely misshapen. I reached for a fresh piece of paper as Kit watched me.

"You actually like her," he said, a small grin breaking free across his wide mouth and making his arrow-lip piercing wiggle. "Oh, well this changes things."

"I never said I liked her."

"You didn't have to." He looked far too smug as he leaned back in his chair, slipping his hands onto the back of his head as his blue hair flopped messily onto his forehead.

I studiously ignored him as I sketched another two

vague figures before adding in some smaller details like the shape of Bryn's mouth and the length of her hair—

My eyes slipped closed. "So what if I like her? What do I do?"

Kit's eyes softened as he leaned in close. "Exactly what you're already doing. Be her friend, be there for her, and, so help me, if you ever hurt her I'll—" He frowned, failing to come up with something suitably threatening. "I don't know, but it'll be bad."

I bit my lip against a smile. Kit was probably one of the least intimidating people I knew—he was like a ball of sunshine, or a hit of pure positive energy.

"I'll bear that in mind," I said dryly and he nodded, clearly pleased he'd done his brotherly duty. "So what's going on with you and Leo?" His mouth dropped open and it was my turn to smirk. "What, you think Bryn only gossips to you?"

"There's nothing going on between me and Leo," Kit said quickly.

"Oh, so he's available then? I was thinking about setting him up with—"

"No," he growled and I smirked. "No, he's not available."

"Interesting," I said, stretching the word out and laughing when Kit grumbled under his breath.

"Ugh, fine. Give that here, watching you struggle is hurting my inner artist."

I happily handed the paper off to him and watched with awe as he shaped the mini versions of younger him and Bryn, smiling with their arms around each other as they ate ice cream. I made grabby hands and he stopped me as I reached for the watercolors.

"I don't want to re-draw that a million times, let me photocopy it and you can practice on the copies. Okay?"

He had a point. "Sounds good."

Kit grabbed the paper and headed over to a chunky white machine in the corner of the room while I waited semi-patiently. Up until that point, I'd never been into any of the art rooms on campus, but they were surprisingly well-stocked and spacious. One or two other students had been in and out fetching supplies while we'd been in there, but for the most part we had the square table to ourselves.

The machine spat out several pieces of paper and Kit brought them over to me before arranging the paints and starting to mix some with a pot of water he'd collected when we'd first sat down.

"Now, you don't want to oversaturate the paper too much. A little bit of bleed is fine and part of the style, but if you soak it too much it'll break or go crispy." I nodded as he demonstrated on a small square of paper. "You know, I'm probably not even the best person to show you this stuff. It's been ages since I did this kind of art, I study graphics."

"Well you know more than me," I pointed out and he snorted.

"I don't think either of us will be winning any fine art awards."

I picked up the brush and immediately splotched paint where I didn't want it. "Ah."

"Yeah, that can happen too."

I tried again and frowned at the smeared mess I made that turned the sketched outlines into shapeless blobs. "I think I've got my work cut out for me."

"Practice makes perfect." Kit playfully swatted at my shoulder and I protested loudly as he jogged my hand. "Bryn won't care that it's not perfect, she'll just be happy you tried."

"Experiences over stuff," I murmured and a gentle look came over his face, softening his eyes and smile.

"Exactly."

CHAPTER THIRTEEN

"WE'RE GOING OUT TONIGHT," BRYN ANNOUNCED two days later as she marched into my room. "Wear something nice."

"How nice?"

"Hoping-you-get-laid, nice."

I swallowed harshly as I looked into her blue eyes. Was she saying...?

"Be ready by six." Without giving me the chance to ask any questions, she swept out of the room as quickly as she'd entered it.

I checked the time. Four. That gave me two hours to do my might-have-sex prep and make myself pretty. It was going to be cutting it fine. Luckily I'd shaved my underarms and legs yesterday, so all I really had to do was exfoliate and tidy downstairs.

I jumped into the bathroom while it was free and turned the water up to near-scalding, my favorite way to shower. After a good forty-minutes of primping and washing and shaving, I emerged feeling absolutely glorious. I'd been sculpted to within an inch of my life— now I just needed to find a good outfit.

I decided to do my make-up first and then just match my clothes to that. I looked at my favorite palette of glittery colors but instead opted for the grungier set Jamie had got for me after insisting I looked 'hot' with a smokey eye.

I blended on reds, silvers and blacks, until I looked like a dark Valentine ready to fulfill all your desires, and then I searched for an outfit.

I settled on a gauzy, floaty dress in dark red to match my eyeshadow and paired it with chunky heels. I felt like a badass. Heck, I *looked* like a badass.

I checked the time and was pleased that I'd managed to get ready with twenty minutes still to spare—but then I noticed the box on the bed. It had a note stuck to it and my belly dipped and tightened as I read it.

Wear me.

It was the present Bryn had given me. I hadn't opened the box yet but the seal was now broken, and when I checked inside I could see the remote was gone.

Wear me. Hoping-you-get-laid nice.

Oh fuck. I breathed in deeply and then slowly let it out as wetness pooled at my center in anticipation.

Did Bryn have the remote? What was she planning to do?

I pulled the inner plastic casing out of the box and hesitantly picked up the small-ish pink egg. It had a soft, silicone-y texture and I stood there for a second debating before I reached under the hem of my dress and pulled my underwear down.

I pressed the egg against my center and felt my clit pulse in response. My body wanted to grind down, wanted release, but this wasn't about that. Not yet, anyway.

The instructions had said *wear me*, so I slid it down over my entrance and pushed it in once I felt like it was wet enough. I gasped, grabbing hold of the edge of the desk as I spread my legs wider.

Jesus, and Bryn wanted me to wear this out of the house? The way it slid around inside me had my toes curling and I wasn't sure I'd be able to get through dinner in this state. I panted for a second, fighting to stay in control, when a knock came at my bedroom door.

"You ready?"

Bryn.

I breathed out slowly, fixed my dress and then opened the door to find her waiting for me in a little black dress that showed off almost as much thigh as I'd seen over at the lake. Lace framed her breasts and small panels on the velvet material to emphasize her figure, she looked like sin and temptation and my mouth went dry as I let my eyes linger on her curves.

She looked perfectly collected, not even blinking as she took me in. If she had the remote, she wasn't going to show it.

I stepped out of my room and into the hall, brushing past her deliberately and didn't even attempt to hide the flush I could feel in my cheeks or the heat in my eyes. If we were going to play this game then fine. Point, set, match.

"Where are we going?"

"Dinner," was all she said, texting someone on her phone and I couldn't have replied even if I'd wanted to because the egg started vibrating. It was clearly on the lowest setting, a barely perceptible tingle that made me want to squirm. It was enough to make my hands clench, to keep me on the edge, but not enough to make me fall.

"You alright?"

I looked at her for a long moment, my face carefully blank and met her own cultivated stare. "Of course."

She nodded and we set off out of the apartment and through the strip of bars until we took a turn that was familiar. It was the same italian place I'd been to with the redhead Bryn had set me up with. A date then. It had to be. But why all the secrecy?

It was cozy inside, the lighting brighter than candlelit but still warm, and the smell of garlic bread had my stomach grumbling. Bryn smiled at the hostess who led us to a roomy booth in the corner of the room. The table and benches were all solid dark wood, cushioned with olive green fabric and deep purple pillows. How had I not appreciated it the last time I'd come here? I glanced at Bryn, busy on her phone again. I suspected my current company had something to do with how present I now was, everything felt heightened around her.

I'd just got settled when the egg seemed to crank up a notch, making my leg twitch under the table and knock into Bryn's.

"Sorry," I murmured. "Leg cramp."

Her eyes flashed and I bit my lip, not willing to be the first to lose face. I casually looked over the menu but my eyes slid shut when another increased vibration seemed to be flowing through me in waves that made my hips want to rock. A bead of sweat slid down my back and I clenched my hands around the faux leather booklet. I would not beg for relief. Or pleasure.

Bryn watched me carefully, noting the determination on my face, and a slow smile spread across her lips that baffled me.

Then the hostess was back, with two people in tow.

"Now you're all here, I'll be back in a moment to get your drinks order." She beamed at us and I watched in shocked silence as Jamie and Ryan joined us.

I said a quick hello and then lapsed into silence as I tried to focus on the menu and not the sensations that were slowly driving me insane.

"Liv's eaten here before, so maybe she can recommend something good," Bryn said cheerfully and I glared.

"Actually, we come here a lot." Ryan smiled at Jamie and I watched them curiously, waiting for a surge of bitterness that never came. "We had our first proper date here."

"Oh yeah, he brought you flowers," I said absently as I looked over the menu for the hundredth time.

The hostess came back and I couldn't have said what I ordered. Not when the vibrations of the toy had reached a new high and I was barely keeping it together.

"Are you okay?" Jamie leaned across the table to look at me, concern pinching her eyes. "You look a little red."

"And sweaty," Bryn added and I wanted to hit her. Or kiss her. Or pin her to my bed and ride her face until—

"I'm fine," I practically snarled. "It's just a little hot in here."

I just had to get through this one meal. I could do this.

Our food came out and I concentrated on picking up the fork and mechanically putting it in my mouth. I was pretty sure it was bolognese, but it was hard to appreciate it when my thighs were clenched together so hard it was almost painful. I contributed to the conversation as little as possible, until it was unavoidable.

"So Jay says you're leaving your course?" Ryan's big blue eyes peered at me gently and I realized that to a psych major I probably looked insane right now.

"Yeah, I hate it." I laughed sharply and bit it off when the toy swapped from constant vibrations to an intermittent pulse that made me curl my hand around my drink for a second before I looked back to Ryan. "Sorry, what was I saying? Oh, yeah. The course isn't for me. Bryn's been helping me work out where my interests might lie instead."

"Oh really?" He looked between us and then raised half a brow at Jamie—did he think I couldn't see him? "What sort of things have you guys been doing?"

The flash of amusement on Bryn's face was so fast I almost missed it as she opened her mouth. "Well—"

I cut her off. "We went skinny dipping, I bought some scary lingerie, I had my first driving lesson, and I smoked a joint. Oh, and I might be training to work at the animal shelter."

"That's great," Ryan said, his eyes lighting up.

"Sounds productive." Jamie smirked and I didn't respond other than to flip her off.

"You're seeing your parents soon though, right?"

I re-focused on Ryan. "Yeah. Bryn's coming to that too, seeing as it was her idea for me to agree to it."

"Seems fair." His lip twitched and I slumped slightly as the toy finally went dormant.

I shrugged and ignored the way Jamie kept glancing back and forth between me and Bryn, until she stood up abruptly and we all looked at her in confusion.

She dropped some cash on the table and tugged at Ryan's arm. "Sorry guys, emergency came up and we have to go."

I raised an eyebrow. She hadn't even checked her phone, I tried to protest but the toy restarted full force and I nearly bit my tongue off. I glared at Bryn and she smirked back at me, not even bothering to pretend any more. By the time I looked up, Jamie was already walking away but she glanced back to look between Bryn and I meaningfully with a quick grin.

Damn it. She was trying to leave us alone together. But if Bryn wanted that, she wouldn't have invited them in the first place—or maybe she was just trying to torture me.

I pointedly ignored her, turning to the side of garlic bread I hadn't even touched yet.

"You did so good." There was a purr in her voice I'd never heard before.

"No thanks to you," I muttered and she laughed quietly.

"I meant with Jamie and Ryan, you didn't even care that they were here together did you?"

I shrugged and glanced up to see Bryn on her phone. "Who do you keep texting?"

Blue eyes danced with mischief as they looked up and met mine. "Remote app."

I shivered as the toy started pulsing faster, like it was spinning or something, and an involuntary groan slipped out of my mouth.

"I'm not going to leave your list unfinished, Olivia."

Oh God. She was really doing this here. *Have an orgasm in public.*

"And you held out for so long." Her hand touched my knee under the table and just that small contact sent tingles running up and down my leg. "So if you beg me, I'll let you come now."

Sweat was starting to pool beneath my breasts as I sat there, trying desperately not to move my hips, but my breaths were coming faster and I felt out of control, like I would have done anything to just meet that final crest.

Bryn's fingertips brushed higher and I slumped back in my seat, glad that our booth was near the back of the restaurant and relatively secluded as her fingers brushed my underwear and found them soaked.

"Just say the word," she murmured as her featherlight

strokes continued to tease me in sync with the toy inside me, "and I'll make you come, Liv."

One more pass of her fingers and my hips rocked up. I looked into her face and saw only hunger, desire, as she wet her lips. "Yes."

"Yes what?"

"*Bryn.*"

"Say it."

"I need you," I panted as my own wetness started to leak out, making my thighs slick. "Make me come." It was a demand, pure and simple, and Bryn's smile was full of promise as her fingers slid under my underwear and into my pussy, rocking into me in a motion that had me biting my lip against a shout as she brushed against the toy. I could no longer tell what was the toy pulsing and what was my pussy as she slid her fingers free and instead bore down on my clit. My spine curled and her free hand reached across the table to cover my mouth as I came.

"The next time I make you come," Bryn said as she leaned back against the booth, "I want the whole world to know my name from your lips."

My legs were shaking and the room felt a little fuzzy by the time I convinced my eyes to open again. Bryn looked ridiculously smug as she wiped her glistening fingers on a napkin and then wrapped the egg up in a spare one that she dropped into her purse.

"Dessert?" the waitress asked, seeming to appear out of nowhere, and Bryn raised a taunting eyebrow at me.

"Oh, no thanks. I'm not sure we'll be able to walk home at this rate."

The waitress laughed but I gave Bryn a shrewd look. Yeah, she may have won the battle, but I was the one who'd had the ridiculously good orgasm. So who was really the winner here?

"Are you ready to get out of here?" she asked after she paid and I nodded. "I hope you had a good time."

I smiled faintly. "I'm a little concerned that I had a better time than you."

She shook her head. "Definitely not, I'm feeling highly satisfied." She grinned at me and I grabbed my jacket as we made our way outside.

Was this like the kiss? Were we going to ignore this had ever happened? Did she want more? I opened my mouth to ask but then closed it again. What did *I* want? A few weeks ago, I probably wouldn't have taken the time to ask myself that question and I partially had Bryn to thank for that.

So instead of bogging down the evening with heavier talk, I just looped my arm through hers and enjoyed the air as we walked back to the apartment. By the time we made it back there, I'd changed my mind—I couldn't just leave things up in the air like this. She'd offered before to help me, as my *friend*, so I'd be more comfortable when I ticked that off the list. Was that all this had been?

But the way she'd looked at me...The way she'd touched me—that didn't feel like *just friends*.

"Are we going to talk about it?" I said quietly as we walked inside.

"Talk about what?" she said calmly and I stared at her back as she brushed past me and into the living room.

"The fact that you had your fingers inside of me less than twenty minutes ago?"

She paused.

"What is there to say?"

I don't know. A lot? I wanted to say but bit my tongue. "I see." It had meant something to me, but not to her. Whatever *this* was, she didn't want it to happen again. "Night, then."

She didn't stop me and I didn't look back. It felt like something had changed, like a choice had been made, but I didn't know if it had been me or her that had done the choosing—and whether or not it was the right decision, I had no idea.

CHAPTER FOURTEEN

JAMIE LET US BORROW HER CAR AGAIN FOR THE drive down to see my parents and the vibe felt very different to when we'd gone down to the lake. Luckily, my parents weren't too far away but they were still a good couple of hours in the car and I opted to fill the silence with music rather than talk. We weren't ignoring what had happened, exactly, it was more that I didn't think either of us were sure what to do with it.

Did I like Bryn? Sure. Was I in-like with Bryn? I thought so. But did she like me? Well, the other night definitely seemed promising until she'd dismissed it. Really I just wanted to focus on getting through this dinner and visit more than working out what Bryn and I were or weren't.

"It's this one on the left," I said over the sound of Taylor Swift as we pulled onto my parent's street.

Bryn parked up and we sat there for a second, her eyes on my face. "Are you ready for this?"

I lifted one shoulder. "Yeah, I guess. Thanks for coming with me."

"Of course," she said softly and we got out of the car. It felt very nostalgic, standing in front of their house—*my house*—as an outsider looking in. I genuinely hadn't thought I would ever be here again. When they'd walked away from me before, it had hurt like hell, but I'd accepted it. I'd tried to move on. But now, here I was again, potentially opening myself back up just to get hurt again.

Bryn squeezed my hand in wordless support and I took a deep breath as I walked up the porch to knock on the door. My dad answered and I was relieved by that, I'd already seen him recently so I was prepared for it. But my mother...

He seemed to read the question on my face as he drew me into a hug that I didn't quite return before he quickly let me go and, to my surprise, hugged Bryn too. "She's in the kitchen, finishing up the food."

I nodded and he took our bags upstairs. I hovered awkwardly in the hall for a second before shrugging off my coat and pulling my glasses out of my pocket. It was the smallest concession I was willing to make, considering I needed to wear them anyway. Bryn stared at me and I frowned.

"What?"

"You look so fucking hot right now," she murmured and I blushed.

"Olivia?"

I turned and there she was. "Hi, Mom."

My mother was a beautiful woman. She'd aged

gracefully and everything about her, from her make-up to her clothes, screamed *tasteful*. This was not a woman who was used to anything less than perfection.

I tugged on my shirt sleeves and then gave her the best smile I could manage under the circumstances. "This is Bryn."

Her green eyes flitted to Bryn behind me and she smiled. I supposed Bryn counted as a guest, so only the best southern hospitality would do. We hadn't grown up in the south, and my mom had moved away when she was a teenager, but some of her own mother's teachings around guests in the home still lingered today.

"Well? Aren't you going to say hello?"

I jumped, startled into action as I hurried forward and pressed a kiss to her cheek as I hugged her lightly. I pulled away faster than she probably wanted, but being here in this place had me slipping back into old patterns already. I didn't want to lose the person I was becoming. Bryn held out her hand once I let go and my mom took it before guiding us into the dining room.

"The food's nearly ready, so Bryn won't you take a seat? Olivia, I could use some help bringing the food out."

I nodded, following her into the kitchen and was unsurprised when she stopped me with a hand on my arm. I looked at her warily, wondering what she wanted to say to me in private that she wouldn't say in front of Bryn.

"I'm sorry I couldn't come down to see you before, sweetheart. I was busy working."

Was that it? I nodded. "No worries." I made to turn away and the hand on my arm tightened.

"I need you to know, that I've been doing a lot of work." Was she bragging? Was this going to turn into a lecture into my own work ethic? "On myself," she added and looked at me expectantly.

My brow furrowed as I thought over her words. "Am I here because you want me to be? Or because this is some kind of step in a programme?"

"Don't be crass." She rolled her eyes and I shrank back. "I just wanted you to know that despite everything that happened with that... woman, we forgive you."

I felt slightly queasy as I looked into her earnest-eyes. "How big of you," I managed and she nodded with a small smile, clearly not sensing my sarcasm. Nothing had really changed, regardless of what my dad said or what they were telling themselves. Maybe on that fundamental level, people just couldn't change. I had been an idiot for letting Bryn talk me into this.

I took the dish she was holding out and brought it into the dining room, numb. I must have looked slightly dazed because Bryn was half way out of her seat by the time I reached the table.

"What's wrong? What happened?"

I motioned for her to sit down as I set the dish on the silver placemat in the center. The smell of it finally hit me and my stomach growled. Lasagna. My mother's recipe.

"It's fine."

Bryn frowned as she slowly sat back down and I slipped into my own seat, back ramrod straight.

My dad made his way down the stairs, footsteps quiet against the light gray carpet, and headed straight into the kitchen to retrieve a stack of dishes that he put delicately onto each place setting.

"Sit, sit, sit," my mom fussed as she walked into the room with another plate full of garlic bread and we all did as instructed as she served up the food. "You're not a veggie are you, Bryn?"

"No, ma'am."

"Oh, please. Call me Melissa."

I grimaced and took a sip of water to cover it before passing my plate over so she could dish some lasagna up. "It looks great, Mom."

"I know it's your favorite," she said with a smile and I looked away from her, instead focusing on the cream embossed-floral wallpaper opposite me that had been up since I was a kid. "So your dad told me you're definitely leaving Radclyffe?"

I nodded. "Yes. I've applied to be a trainee at the local shelter, I'm just waiting to hear back."

My mom laughed and then blinked. "Oh, you're serious."

I clenched my jaw, knowing that I would probably be replaying the derision in that laugh over and over again in my head for the next few days. Bryn's eyes met mine, concern evident on her face as she watched me. I shook my head at her slightly. It was fine. This was fine.

I automatically took my dad's hand to my right and my mother's on my left, ready for grace and then cleared my throat. "Ah, Bryn, you don't have to—"

"I don't mind," she said, reaching for my parent's hands and listening intently when they began their prayer.

"Thank you for allowing us to grow, to heal, and let us all join together here today to become a strong, loving family again. Amen." My dad's voice was a comforting rumble but I wanted to laugh. Grow and heal? Become strong and loving again? The only thing that had become stronger, as far as I could tell, was my mother's propensity to buy her own bullshit.

"What do you study, Bryn?" My dad smiled as he reached for some garlic ciabatta, clearly trying to steer the conversation into safer waters.

"I'm training to be a lawyer."

"That's wonderful," my dad mumbled around his food and my mom frowned at him before turning her attention to Bryn.

"See, Olivia? A proper degree and a proper aspiration. Maybe Bryn will be a good influence on you."

I couldn't help it, I started to laugh. Considering Bryn made me orgasm in the middle of a restaurant less than two days ago, I felt pretty confident that she wasn't my mom's idea of a 'good influence'.

"Olivia..." My dad said warningly and I fell silent.

"I don't think one career path is more valid than the other," Bryn said, looking at my mother head on as I froze.

"Then you're as foolish as my daughter, she always did make poor choices when it came to the women in her life."

I snapped. I'd had *enough*. I'd come here to give them one more chance, but everything was the same. My mom was like poison and my dad would agree with her to his dying breath. I couldn't go back to the way things were before. I *liked* who I was now, or who I was becoming at least. "No."

My mom's fork stopped half-way up to her mouth as she looked at me. "No?"

"No," I repeated more slowly and, in that moment, I decided to pretend I was Jamie. She'd constantly shocked me with her strength, her propensity to cut with words, and I couldn't be soft right now. Otherwise I'd never get out of here. "Do you need me to spell it for you?"

"Olivia," my dad gasped as Bryn coughed to hide a laugh.

"Now listen here, young lady—"

"No," I repeated with a shrug as I set my cutlery down and stood. "I don't have to listen to you. I've been doing more than fine without you in my life and the last thing I need is you spouting some faux-sincere bullshit as you preach to me about how much you've changed."

I didn't even realize I was breathing hard until I stopped talking. Bryn stood too and gestured to me that she was going upstairs. I was confused for a second until I remembered that my dad had taken our bags up there. I nodded and she left quickly.

"You haven't changed," I continued as I looked between my parents. "You're just as awful as you ever were and I don't want to see you again."

"Is it her?" My mother demanded as she rose from her seat to glare at me. "The blonde you brought with you. Is it her that's corrupted you like this?"

I snorted. "If you mean did Bryn make me come in a restaurant full of people, take me skinny dipping, smoke some weed with me for the first time, and give me my first driving lesson—then yes, she corrupted me and *I liked it*."

They gaped at me as I neatly tucked in my chair and made my way to the door of the dining room before I stopped. "You're both as toxic as you ever were. Fire your therapist, because they're clearly terrible at their job."

I walked out and found Bryn waiting for me at the front door.

"You okay?" she said as I slammed it behind us.

I thought about it for a second before I nodded. "Surprisingly, yes. I said everything I needed to and more."

Bryn tugged me to a stop as we reached her car, taking my bags from me and then looking deeply into my eyes. "You were amazing back there. You should be proud of yourself, Liv."

"I am." I smiled as I took a deep breath of the cool evening air. "I really, really am."

We climbed back into the car and Bryn grimaced as she settled behind the wheel. "Do you mind if we stop somewhere for the night? I've just already done a lot of driving today and—"

"Of course," I interrupted. "Let me look up what's around." It wasn't late, but I felt like the day had been emotionally draining—dealing with asshole parents tended to have that effect. "Okay..." I said as I flicked through my phone. "There's a pretty nice hotel about ten minutes away? We might as well sleep in style, right?"

Bryn chuckled. "I think you've earned it."

I flopped back onto the bed and groaned. I'd had maybe two bites of the lasagna at my mom's before we'd left, so once we'd checked into this—admittedly outrageously expensive—hotel, we'd splashed out on room service and now I wasn't sure I could move.

Bryn laid back next to me and we stared at the high ceiling together, the television the only sound in the room as my thoughts swirled around my head like the past few hours were only now setting in. I couldn't have anticipated how things would have gone with my parents today, but maybe I should have. Maybe I'd been foolish to hope.

As if she could sense my thoughts from the change in my mood, Bryn rolled over to look at me. "It's not your fault that they were like that today. You gave them a chance, it's their loss that they wasted it."

"I know."

We fell silent and while I didn't feel as low as I had a few weeks back, I still felt like everything was piling up into one giant ball of shit with no way to unravel it. First my confusing, possibly unrequited, feelings for Bryn, then this mess with my parents. It made me feel like an idiot. Even when I tried to do the right thing, make the right choices, I still wound up in a mess bigger than when I started.

A warm hand cupped my cheek and I hadn't realized I

was crying until Bryn brushed the tear away. "It's okay. You can let it out."

"I don't want to."

"You'll feel better if you do."

I held my breath, unwilling to let the pain festering inside escape—because then I would have to confront it, once and for all.

Bryn shuffled closer, wrapping her arms around me so my head was pillowed on her chest as a ragged sob left my lips. I tried to clamp it back and she tutted.

"You need to let this go, Liv. Cry them out. Let the pain dull." Her fingers stroked through my hair and my breaths followed the lull of her hands, stuttering in and out faster and faster.

It was like an unleashing, like my soul was seizing inside my body as it purged itself of the shame, the worry, the *fear*.

"You're enough," Bryn murmured as I shook. "You're everything."

My breathing finally slowed as my tears ran out, and my eyes fluttered open to find Bryn's already on mine.

"Okay?" she said and I nodded, licking my lips as I felt the warmth of her body easing into mine.

"Thank you."

She shook her head. "You don't need to—"

"I do."

We both went quiet, our eyes holding as the space between us seemed to shrink. We'd shared a bed before, several times now, but it had never felt like this. This was like playing with fire and hoping you got burned, or taking the plunge and not bothering with a parachute. Dangerous. Free fall.

"What are we doing here, Bryn?"

She blinked and it felt like electricity was coursing through my veins, my heart beating quicker now that I'd dared to voice one of the questions I so desperately needed answered: *Did she want me as much as I wanted her?*

"We're two friends. In bed."

The word 'bed' seemed to hang between us like a promise and despite her words, it felt like she moved closer.

"Friends."

"Yeah," Bryn said breathlessly, her chin tilting upwards ever so slightly.

"In bed."

"Right," she murmured, eyes dipping down to watch my mouth and the next time I spoke, her lips brushed across mine.

"Just. Friends."

She kissed me and my breath was lost as my lungs filled with the scent of her. This. This was what I'd been waiting for, what I'd needed—to be lost in the sensation of the touch of her mouth, the sound of her gasp as our tongues met.

"Bryn..." I didn't need to say anything else. Her hand slid into my hair, tugging like she'd never get me close enough, and her lips tasted mine like they were never meant to be apart. She was warm, so so warm, and when I trailed my lips down the side of her throat it was her turn to pant for me.

My hand skimmed her side, cupping her hip as her mouth moved lower. My chest rose sharply to meet her lips as I gasped and when her tongue licked a path across the tops of my breasts I whimpered, desperate for her.

"Maybe..." I gasped as her warm hand touched the bare skin of my waist under my shirt. "Maybe we should slow down a little."

Bryn's hand fell away as she rolled onto her back and I bit my lip, worried I'd made a mistake or that she thought I was pushing her away.

"I didn't mean—"

"No, it's okay. I understand." She wouldn't look at me, her gaze focused studiously on the ceiling before she abruptly stood and moved away from the bed. "I'm going to shower or something," she muttered and I opened my mouth but no words came out before the door to the bathroom closed behind her with a gentle *click*.

The sound of the water filled the room and I watched the door intently, thinking she would be out soon and we could talk this out. When I'd said we should slow down, I hadn't meant that I regretted kissing her, or anything that followed. But I didn't want to do whatever it was we were doing until I knew what it meant.

I picked up my phone with a sigh and found several messages in the group chat from Jamie and Kat, asking how today had gone, and I dropped them a quick update before assuring them I was fine. Jamie, typically, summarized her feelings with a heartfelt *fuck 'em* and Kat sent me a bunch of love hearts—I wasn't sure how I'd ended up with such good friends, but I was grateful nonetheless.

At some point I couldn't put my finger on, things had shifted for me. I would always love Jamie, but more as a sister than anything else. What I felt for Bryn was wholly different. New and fresh, *ours*—if only she could sit down and listen to me long enough to let me make her mine.

CHAPTER FIFTEEN

"To be clear, you've decided to formally withdraw?" Winters couldn't have looked more surprised if she'd tried—mostly because she'd drawn on her eyebrows slightly too high—but I nodded anyway.

"I really appreciate Radclyffe and the course making room for me as a late starter, but it's just not a good fit."

"Well." She coughed lightly. "If you're sure, I'll alert the student management team and they'll email you the papers."

"That's great, thank you." I smiled and she returned it, so at least there were no bridges burned. Who knew what the future held, after all.

I left Winters' office feeling like a weight had been lifted. Even with things still up in the air between Bryn and me, I couldn't help but feel like things were finally coming together. I'd fallen asleep long before Bryn had emerged from the hotel bathroom and she'd silenced any attempt at conversation on the drive home by blasting music.

It was still relatively early out, I wasn't sure why the faculty insisted on holding these meetings in the morning —some of us liked to sleep in. I smiled as I started through the park, once those papers were finalized I could sleep in as much as I wanted.

Though, considering I'd heard back from May yesterday and she'd offered me the traineeship at the shelter, maybe I wouldn't be getting as many chilled mornings as I otherwise would have. I bit my lip to hold back the smile that wanted to break out at the thought, not wanting to look weird as I strolled through the park on the way to my first proper shift.

I was nervous, but this felt like a good decision and I knew as soon as I got back in there with the animals I'd feel calmer.

May smiled from the doorway of the shelter as she waved a young couple outside, cat carrier in hand as they made their way to a small blue car. "Morning!"

"Hey." I wiped my slightly-sweaty hands on my jeans and gave her a nervous smile in return. "New owners?"

May nodded as I walked in and let the door close behind me. "Yep, little Marshmallow found her forever home."

I was both happy and sad to hear that, I'd only seen the cat once and I'd already become attached.

May passed me a new shirt with the shelter's logo on the front and had me fill out a few forms before we headed to the back to check on the cats. She handed me the small gray kitten I'd seen on my first day here and I cradled her in my arms delicately while she purred.

"This little one has a little cold, so we've got some meds for her. It's quite common for kittens to get upper respiratory infections."

I nodded. "Yeah, I read that online," I murmured as I held the kitten's head still so May could give her the antibiotic paste. "Does she have a name yet?"

"Not yet, I was thinking I might wait for her people to name her—kittens tend to go quickly."

Something about that bothered me and May noticed. It wasn't quite jealousy, it was more...*protectiveness*.

"Surely it might be better though," I said slowly, "if the person looking after her knew what they were doing? You know, like if they knew how to give her this medicine."

"Hmm, yes I can see your point..." May struggled to hide her smile as I looked down at the ball of warm fluff in my arms and shifted a hand out from under her to stroke gently under her chin.

"I suppose she would need a lot of stuff though..." I frowned but the thought was quickly forgotten as the kitten purred louder the longer I stroked her. "...but maybe there's room..."

"We do give a care package to our clients, I could show you if you like." May raised an eyebrow as she watched the kitten stretch happily in my arms before settling down again. "Just as part of your training, of course."

"Of course," I murmured, only half-listening as I followed her. All my attention stayed on the sleepy sweetie in my arms who had begun softly snoring. "Oh wow," I said as May pulled open a storage cupboard to show me the bags of food, toys, blankets and more that she had stocked inside. "You give all this away for free?"

"It's included in the adoption fee."

"Right." I cleared my throat as the kitten stirred and licked my arm. "How much is that again?"

"Two-hundred for cats, three-hundred for dogs."

I tickled the kitten's tummy when she stretched again and it took me a good few minutes to look up and realize May was still standing there, watching me. "Um, sorry. Did you say something?"

"I said, let's get you rung up."

"Oh, no. No, I couldn't."

"You don't have the room?"

"Well, I—"

"Or you're too busy for the commitment?"

"No, I just—"

"You'd rather she went to someone else?"

"No," I said somewhat sharply and then glanced down, my gaze ensnared again by the kitten. "Ky," I decided, smiling at May. "Her name is Ky. Short for Valkyrie."

"I love it." May nodded approvingly and I laughed breathlessly as I jiggled Ky in my arms. Mine. She was *mine*. "I own a cat," I said wonderingly and May laughed.

"Almost, anyway. You can bring her back here with you when you work if you like, so we can keep an eye on her together."

I signed the contract she held out with a quick glance

over it and reached below the desk to pull my card out of my bag. "Then let's make it official."

We stored the forms away in a locked cabinet beneath the desk before we took Ky back out to the kitten pen and left her there until I finished my shift.

"I can't wait to tell Bryn."

"You two will make excellent moms."

I blushed. "Oh, we're—we're not together."

"Sounds like you've got your work cut out for you then," May said with a wink and I snorted.

"You have no idea."

Kit and Leo met me after my shift, pulling up outside and honking once as if I couldn't see the light blue truck out of the window of the shelter.

"Hey," I called as I stepped outside, my arms full of kitten supplies. "Little help?"

Leo hurried around the side of his truck to grab some stuff and place it in the back. "Um, when you asked us to meet you here, I didn't realize you would have an animal with you."

"Don't worry, Ky's in a carrier."

"Ky?" Leo said, eyebrows rising and Kit looked intrigued.

"If *Ky* poops in Leo's car, he's likely to have a

coronary, just so you know," he muttered to me as I shoved the rest of the kitten supplies onto the back seat.

I rolled my eyes as I turned away and headed back inside the shelter to collect Ky. "I'll see you in a couple of days then, May?"

"Looking forward to it."

I cooed at Ky in her carrier as I pulled open the door, the cool air sneaking in and making her dark eyes fly wide as she huddled at the back of her blankets.

"Is that.... a kitten?" Leo hesitantly peered inside, his blonde hair waving in the slight breeze and Kit brushed Leo's hair back absently as he smiled at Ky.

"Yep, and she's *mine.*" I knew my grin was likely taking up the majority of my face and showing off all my teeth, but I didn't care. I'd started the day by dropping out of college and I'd finished it with a successful first shift at what was rapidly becoming my dream job, as well as a brand new kitten to look after.

"Bryn is going to freak out, she loves cats." Kit gave me a shrewd look and I rolled my eyes.

"I did this for me, not her. But I'm glad it won't drive her away."

"Speaking of things that aren't romantic gestures," Kit said with a roll of his eyes as Leo moved to the driver's side. "How's the artwork coming along?"

I'd spent all weekend pretending that Bryn wasn't avoiding me as I practiced painting the copies Kit had sketched for me and had finally settled on one that didn't look as awful as the others.

"Good," I summarized as I climbed into the car.

"Jamie's?" Leo asked, looking at me in his rearview as I stuck my finger through the bars so Ky could sniff me.

"Yeah, thanks." Oh, crap. That was one thing I hadn't considered—would Jamie care that I'd brought Ky home? I mean, chances were that she wouldn't be home enough to really notice, but still. I gnawed on my bottom lip as we drove the short distance between the mall and the apartment and Kit helped me carry things upstairs.

"Do you think Jamie will be mad?"

"Isn't Jamie always mad?" Leo muttered and I choked on an unexpected laugh as I tried to keep Ky's carrier as still as possible when we walked up the stairs.

We lugged the stuff inside and set her up in the living room. I hadn't ever set up a litter tray before, but after searching online it seemed pretty simple.

I opened the door to the carrier and Ky instantly ran out and hid under the sofa, peeking out at us with big eyes.

"Hey," I called to Kit as I stood up and moved to the hall entrance, "can I talk to you for a sec? Will you watch the kitten please, Leo?"

Leo nodded and Kit followed me into my room, stopping short of my desk when he saw what sat atop it.

"What do you think? Will she like it?" I figured it would be good to show another human before I presented the artwork to Bryn. If Kit visibly recoiled, then I would know to burn it.

Kit lifted the thick paper carefully, examining it closely before he smiled, the piercing in his tongue flashing in the light. "I think she'll love it."

I felt relieved knowing that he approved, and he watched that emotion cross my face, nodding slightly. It may not have started out as a romantic gesture, but it had kind of ended up that way.

We sat back down in the living room and watched TV and chatted while we waited for the kitten to come out from under the sofa. She'd only ventured one paw out from beneath by the time Bryn got home.

She stopped short when she saw Kit and Leo on the sofa sitting with me, her eyebrows quirking up. "Is this an intervention?" Then she noticed all the extra stuff we'd piled into the corner and the litter tray by the window. "What is going on?" Before I could say anything, a streak of gray ran out from under the sofa and twined around her legs and Bryn melted before our eyes. "Oh my god."

"She came out!" I squealed and then clamped a hand over my mouth when Ky shied away. Bryn scooped her up into her arms and stroked her head under her chin.

"Who is this?"

"Ky."

"She's *yours*? Isn't this the kitten from the shelter?"

"May thought we would be a good fit," I said, somewhat defensively.

"Holy shit." Bryn smiled when Ky licked her hand and brought her over to me, placing her into my lap. "Why Ky?"

"Short for Valkyrie."

"Obviously." Kit snorted and Leo chuckled. "Why not Val?"

"Because she's a brave kitty warrior, not a bartender."

Bryn rolled her eyes but couldn't resist petting her some more. If it got her to come within five feet of me, then I would take it.

We played with the kitten, tracing a long ribbon back and forth for her to swat, until she fell asleep on my lap, purring. Kit and Leo left just as Jamie walked in and did a double take. I had thought I'd have more time before I'd have to break the news to her.

"I know I'm not here that often, but when did we get a fucking cat?"

I laughed and then immediately stopped when Ky's eyes fluttered open briefly. "Well, you know how I had my first shift at the shelter today?"

Jamie raised her eyebrows. "You already caved?"

"I already caved," I admitted and she snorted before hesitantly walking over to peer at Ky.

I bit my lip against the laugh that wanted to bubble out. I'd never seen her look so unsure of herself.

"Can I touch her?"

"Sure, but she's a little shy."

Jamie stroked a hand over Ky's dark head and her eyes flew wide. "She's so *soft*."

"Yep," I said smugly. Jamie wasn't going to have a problem with her, so that meant... "She's mine."

"What's her name?"

"Ky," I said, tickling under her chin and beaming when she tilted her head back for more.

"Pretty," Jamie murmured and then balked when I lifted the kitten up and handed her over. "What are you—"

"I need to talk to Bryn, and someone needs to watch her."

Jamie glanced back down at Ky and a small smile appeared on her face. "Okay, fine."

I took Bryn's hand in mine and tugged her into my room. She looked bemused when I shut the door and then stepped in front of it.

"Are you avoiding me?"

She sucked in a breath. "I've just been busy sorting things out with my new place. Why would I avoid you?"

"Because we kissed, and it meant something to me, but then you ran off and haven't spoken to me since." The words fell out of my mouth so fast they practically blurred together and Bryn's mouth dropped open.

"You said we should slow down—"

"I'd had kind of a crazy day! I meant that maybe we could just go to bed and pick things up tomorrow, not that I never wanted you to touch me again."

Bryn folded her arms across her chest as she watched me, a smirk curling her mouth. "You *did* like it."

I shook my head and disappointment filled her expression until I strode forward and cupped her face in my hands. "You're an idiot," I said, and kissed her.

She gasped against my mouth and her back hit my closet as her body molded to mine. I tugged on her lip with my teeth and smiled wickedly at the way she groaned.

"Wait, wait," she said and I pulled back, searching her face for any signs of regret and instead found only surprise. "What is *that*?"

Her eyes had found the painting I'd shown to Kit and

I picked it up and handed it to her carefully, trying not to let my sweaty hands touch it too much. "I know you were upset about your photo being ruined, so I recreated it as best I could."

"This is for me?" she said wonderingly as she looked over the photo of her and Kit as lanky teenagers, smiling as they ate ice cream. "*You* made it?"

"Yep," I said proudly. "I mean, Kit helped a little but... Not too bad, right?"

Her eyes were wide as she looked at me. "Why?"

I shrugged. "Thought it would make you happy."

She set it down on the desk again almost reverently, and this time it was her who kissed me.

My breath caught in my chest at the first touch of her mouth and then it felt like everything was a rush—to get closer, to touch and taste more until we were both breathless.

"Do you want me to slow down?" I mumbled between kisses and Bryn laughed as she reached forward and cupped my breast through my top.

"Slow down? I feel like I've been waiting forever."

I laughed with her as I reached for the hem of her tee, pulling it up and over her head before I kissed my way down and over her breasts, mouthing at her nipples through the sheer material until she moaned for me.

I unhooked her bra and bit my lip as my hands finally got to feel her bare skin, soft under my palms. I licked one nipple, sucking it into my mouth as her hands fisted in my hair before sliding lower to unhook my own bra through my top.

I grinned as I pulled away and caught up to her, her eyes darkening to deep pools of blue as she looked at the top half of my naked body.

She reached for me at the same time that I did for her, our chests brushing together and sending shivers of sensation through me as my tongue stroked hers. Bryn pushed down my jeans and I tugged at the zipper on her pants, our hands constantly moving, touching, until we both stood naked and climbed onto the bed.

"You're so beautiful," I whispered as I kissed down her navel and paused between her legs. "Can I?" Bryn nodded and I think if she hadn't I might have died after seeing her but not tasting her. I licked up the inside of her thighs and she squirmed beneath me, but I hadn't forgiven her for the way she'd teased me in the restaurant. Now was time for payback.

I stroked one finger across the outside of her pussy, avoiding her clit and letting her writhe as I continued to kiss her thigh oh-so-close to where she wanted me.

"Olivia," she said warningly and I chuckled, pressing one finger into her wet heat and withdrawing slowly.

"You're so wet for me Bryn." I slid in two fingers and loved the way her hips rocked up, seeking more, needing more.

"I need your mouth," she gasped and I licked a long line from her clit to her pussy.

"Like that?"

"More."

I'd wanted to hold back, to tease her until she couldn't see straight, but there would be time for that later. Right now I wanted to feel her clit pulsing under my tongue as she came on my fingers.

I lowered my mouth and sucked, chuckling when her hands fisted in my pink bed sheets. "Is this what you wanted, baby?" She replied in nonsensical moans and as I rocked my hand in and out of her, she gasped my name. "You wanted this bad, huh? Your pussy is dripping all over my hand." Bryn moaned louder and I pressed my lips to her clit, kissing and licking until her legs were shaking. "Do you like my fingers?" I curled them for emphasis and then withdrew. "Or do you prefer my tongue?" I slid it into her core, lapping up the moisture dripping down as she creamed for me. "Are you getting close, Bryn?"

I looked up at her from between her legs and the pretty flush on her cheeks made me groan as I pushed my tongue back into her. She tasted better than I could have imagined and I knew I would have the taste and scent of her stuck in my head for weeks. There was no way I could give this up. I still wasn't sure what this meant to her, but for me it was everything.

I increased my pace, reaching up to stroke her clit as my tongue pulsed upward inside her and she came, my name a plea on her lips until she slumped down onto the bed.

"Satisfied?" I smirked as I laid back next to her.

"Very," she said sleepily. "But not completely."

I frowned but started to smile as she cupped one of my breasts in her hand, flicking her thumb across the nipple. "You don't need to do that. I'm okay."

"I want to." She sat up and kissed me, her hands

sliding down my body until she pushed her fingers through my wetness. "Do you want this?"

"I want it all," I breathed and she stilled for a second before smiling.

"Then that's what I'll give you."

I gasped as two fingers immediately filled me, stretching my pussy as she rocked them in and out.

"You can take more," she reassured me and I just moaned breathily. "But don't worry, we'll take it slow." Her mouth joined her fingers and I rocked my hips up against her tongue until she pulled away. "I have an idea."

She climbed back up the bed to me and I protested a little until she laid back down and patted my outer thigh. "Come here."

I raised an eyebrow. "I like the way your mind works."

"I thought you might."

I settled myself on her mouth and the first flick of her tongue made me gasp as her hands gripped my ass. "Yes," I panted and she moaned beneath me, making my hips rock faster as I rode her face.

She slid one hand between us, pumping three fingers into my pussy as her tongue worked my clit and I bounced on them eagerly, encouraging her to go deeper, harder. Then I glanced back and noticed the direction of her other hand as she spread her own pussy open and rocked two fingers inside.

I lifted myself off of her mouth, ignoring her whimpered protests as I gripped the hand she'd been using to fuck herself and licked the fingers clean. I lifted her right leg and she bit her lip as she nodded and I settled in between them before moving forward and pressing us together.

Bryn sucked in a breath and my head fell back as our hips circled in sync, the slickness between us growing as my clit brushed hers. We rode each other hard and I felt it when she came again, her pussy quivering under mine and pushing me over the edge as our hips finally stilled.

"You were right," I said to her once I got my breath back. "That was long overdue."

She laughed, just as breathless as me, and I crawled to the top of the bed to lay next to her. "How much of that do you think Jamie heard?"

I snorted. "I really, truly, don't care."

CHAPTER SIXTEEN

Jamie kept smirking at me over breakfast until I finally sighed and said, "What?"

"Just friends, huh?"

I rolled my eyes. "Well, at the time that was true." Bryn and I had spent the remainder of the night curled up watching *The Vampire Diaries* as Ky slept between us. I still needed to talk to her and make sure that we were on the same page—I didn't just want to sleep with her, I wanted her to be mine.

"Is this all part of your little project too? Friends who fuck?"

"Shut up," I muttered as I sipped my OJ and then nearly choked when I saw Bryn standing in the doorway, watching us. "Hi. Morning. Hey." It hadn't been awkward yesterday after we'd had sex, so why did I feel so unsure now?

Jamie raised her eyebrows at me and I opted to ignore her. Yes, I had no cool.

"Sorry, don't let me interrupt." Was I imagining the coldness in Bryn's voice? I looked quickly to Jamie but she raised her shoulders as if to say she was staying out of it.

"You're not interrupting. Do you want some breakfast?"

"No, I'm actually going to head to my new place."

"Oh." What the hell was going on? "Right now? Do you want me to come with you?"

"That's kind of outside the parameters of *friends who fuck*, I think," she said as she turned away.

Crap. "Bryn, that's not—"

The door slammed and I stared at the empty spot she'd occupied just a second ago.

Jamie slapped my arm. "Aren't you going after her?"

I stumbled up and grabbed the first pair of shoes I found, shoving them on as I ran out of the door and then promptly kicking them off when I realized they were platform heels and were hindering more than helping.

"Bryn!" I called out and got no response. Damn. How fast *was* she?

I hurried down the steps and out of the building, probably looking deranged with half a shoe on, bedhead, and my wrinkled PJs completing the look as I yelled for her.

How was she already on the path through the park? She was still in her PJs too, but somehow managed to pull it off as if it were a new trend us mere mortals hadn't yet thought of.

"Bryn!"

She didn't turn and I swore as a pebble cut into my

foot. I veered onto the grass and half-tackled her to get her to stay put.

"Stop! I don't know what you think you heard—"

"Were you just using me last night to make her jealous?"

"What? No. Of course not!"

"Then is this about the list? You—what, got caught up in everything with me? Or felt like you owed me something?"

"Bryn—"

"I already told you once." Her blue eyes were glossy with tears as she stared at me. "I don't want to be someone's second choice. I am *not* a consolation prize. And if you think—"

I kissed her, slamming my mouth onto hers with all the love and irritation and passion I felt before pulling back. "God damn it, will you just stop?"

"I don't want to be a consolation prize," she repeated, eyes shining, and I brushed away the tear that was making its way down her cheek.

"You could never, ever, be a consolation prize." I pulled her to me, holding her tightly before I moved away again so I could meet her eyes. "Bryn, you are... everything."

She looked like she wasn't sure she believed me.

"If you'd just waited, I wouldn't have had to chase you down in my pajamas and half a platform heel." Bryn glanced down at my feet and a wet laugh left her. "I'm playing for keeps. All in. Whatever you can give me, I'll take. I love you."

"But what about Jamie?"

I shook my head as I glanced out at the park. We were garnering a few odd looks but I didn't care. Bryn was too important for me to just let her walk away without all the facts. "Jamie is my friend."

"And that's it?"

"Yes. What I thought I felt for her... Well, it didn't hurt nearly as much as my heart did when you walked away from me. Twice."

Her lips twitched before forming a small smile. "I'm moving out."

I bit my lip, my stomach dropping. "Okay." I had just fucked this whole thing up.

"But I guess I would miss Ky." I nodded slowly, not sure if she was going somewhere or just trying to be mean. "So maybe I don't have to miss her."

"You want to stay?"

"I want you to leave." I hesitated, beyond confused as I obeyed and turned away, stilling only when she caught my arm. "Leave Jamie's, you idiot. Come and live with me. I decided to buy a place, there's plenty of room. We can have our own bedrooms if you like so things don't feel like they're moving too fast."

Bryn was rambling, I realized. She was *nervous*. She wanted me just as much as I wanted her.

"It is a little fast..." I admitted. "But that would be a good change of pace for us."

Her eyes lit up. "You're sure?"

A slow smile broke out on my face. "You want me?"

"More than anything," she murmured. A flush of pink

seared her cheeks and I pressed a kiss to each of them. "There's no rush though. I can move in now and you could join me later..."

I kissed her. "I want to be there with you from the start."

"Really?"

"I feel like we skipped a few stages, but yes." Bryn laughed, the sound tinged with relief, and I kissed her again. "Can we maybe go back inside now? My toes are going to fall off."

We stuck to the grass as we made our way back to the apartment and Bryn pulled me onto her back when we got to the sidewalk so I wouldn't hurt my feet any more. I snagged my shoe from the top of the stairwell and laughed when we walked in and found Jamie still sitting in the same spot.

"All good?" she called and I pulled Bryn into the room with me. She immediately went over to check on Ky and pressed a kiss to her tiny head.

"Yeah," I said and glanced at Bryn, happiness bubbling away inside me. "But, ah, I'm moving out."

"What?" she squealed. "Jesus. You two go big or go home, I guess. You're sure about this?"

"Yes," I said with a small smile, glad she cared enough to check-in.

We all stopped talking to watch Ky do a ridiculously big yawn and coo at her before Jamie turned back to us like she'd just remembered we were having a conversation. "So are you guys like, a couple now?"

I looked at Bryn and found her eyes already on me. "If she'll have me."

Bryn stood and walked over to me, her eyes bright as she pressed a lingering kiss to my lips. "Like I could get rid of you now."

"Wow, PDA much." I shot Jamie a look and she laughed. "No, this is great. I called this from day one, just so you know."

"Aren't you going to miss us?"

"Sure. But I, um—"

"You're going to ask Ryan to move in, aren't you?"

Jamie grinned. "Do you think he'll say yes?"

"You spend all your time together anyway," I said with a roll of my eyes. "I would eat this sweet little kitty cat if he said no," I sang at Ky and she yawned at me.

I straightened up to find them both giving me identical looks of horror.

"I wouldn't actually eat her," I protested and Jamie shook her head slowly at me. "Oh whatever." I held out my hand to Bryn and waited while she gave Ky one last pet before tugging her along to the bathroom. "Let's get ready and then go and see the new place?"

She smiled slowly as she backed me into the bathroom and locked the door. "What's the rush?"

"Did I mention I love you?" I moaned as Bryn stripped me of my clothes and kissed my throat.

"You did."

I raised an eyebrow as I got on my knees. "Do I need to remind you why you love me?"

"Now you're putting words in my mouth."

"I'd rather put something else in there." I smirked when Bryn laughed and let her pull me up off of the floor and into the shower. The water was hot and the company was even hotter, I let my head fall forward and Bryn stroked the soap all over my body, running her hands up and over my shoulders and then slapping my butt before rinsing me off. I returned the favor and by the time we climbed out of the shower, I wanted her again.

She saw the look on my face and swayed her hips deliberately as we made our way back to my room. "I thought you wanted to go and see our new place?"

"In a minute," I said huskily. "It can wait a minute, can't it?"

"Maybe," Bryn said as I stroked one hand over her breast. "I could be persuaded."

I bent my face to her breasts and spent the next few minutes worshiping each of them until she was panting. "Are you wet for me yet?"

Her smile was sly as she backed onto my bed and parted her thighs. "Why don't you check?"

I slid a hand down her stomach and pressed it between her legs as I joined her, rolling her clit in a way that made her breath catch as I moved lower and sank one finger into her pussy.

"You feel so good. So wet."

"Maybe," she said around a moan, "I should check on you too."

I took her hand and placed it between my thighs. "Be my guest."

The first touch of her fingers made me shiver, her

hand deftly working my clit as one finger curled inside me and I gasped. I increased the speed of my hand inside her and shuddered when she did the same for me, two fingers now pumping in and out. Before long, the only sounds in the room were our moans and the wetness of each of us as we raced to finish the other off first.

"Bryn," I gasped, my back arching when her other hand rolled my nipple between her fingers.

"Come for me, Olivia," she demanded and I couldn't hold back, clenching around her fingers as my hips rocked uncontrollably and I felt her pussy contract around mine before I flopped back onto the bed beside her.

For a second we just stopped and breathed and when I finally had the energy to turn my head towards her, she was already looking at me.

"I'm going to make you come in every room of the new place," she said eventually and I smirked.

"Like I would protest that?"

Her laugh joined mine and when we eventually moved to get dressed, it was with frequent pauses for kisses and touches that made it hard to stay focused—not that I was complaining.

"I love you," she said finally, pressing a kiss to my lips as we got dressed and I smiled.

I was going to see my new home today, with my new girlfriend, and my new kitten. Life couldn't get better than that.

EPILOGUE

"Ky, you need to do the pee *in* the litter box," I groaned and she blinked her little eyes at me as I cleaned up the mess she'd made. "You're lucky you're so cute."

Bryn walked into the kitchen and made a face. "Aw, another accident sweetie?"

"To be fair, I think she was aiming for the litter box and just didn't get there in time."

Bryn picked Ky up and stroked along her head before tickling under her chin. "You'll get there, sweetheart."

I smiled, loving watching them together. Ky had settled in so well to the new apartment, aside from a few accidents, and it felt like Bryn and I were following in her tiny footsteps. We were decorating one room at a time with a good mixture of restrained elegance and a riot of color, it was a challenge but one we were both enjoying for now. I had my own room, directly opposite Bryn's, but we spent the majority of both our days and nights together regardless. It was nice to have the option of space though, if we needed it. Things had been a slow-building simmer for us, but once I'd finally managed to make her mine it had all progressed quite quickly. It was working for us though, and that's all that mattered.

Bryn had finished college for the summer and was interning at a local not-for-profit firm which still left plenty of time for us to see each other, whereas I was working at the animal shelter and May let me bring Ky into work with me. It was work I adored, the only problem was that I wanted to adopt every animal in the place. So far, I'd managed to restrain myself but I'd started cooking up a plan to open my own shelter or sanctuary one day. I needed to get more experience first, though I'd learned a lot just from having Ky.

"Um, Liv?"

I glanced up from the dishes I was busy washing and met Bryn's eyes. "Yeah?"

"You know how the paint in the spare room is wet?"

"Sure," I said, scrubbing at a particularly stubborn coffee stain in my favorite mug. "Why?"

"Our kitten is pink."

I stood perfectly still for a second before turning slowly to see what Bryn was talking about. There, all down one side of Ky's fur was a perfect, baby pink patch.

"Crap."

A knock on the door left me torn but Bryn smiled gently as she tossed me the towel to dry my hands. "Go. I'll sort her out."

"Thank you." I kissed her quickly on my way to the

door and double checked she had a hold of Ky before I opened it to find Kat standing there with a manic look in her eyes. "Oh! Hi, everything okay?" I stepped back from the door so she could come in and she immediately began to pace. We hadn't done a proper housewarming yet, though Kat and Jamie had been by a few times to play with Ky, and it felt like Kit was here most days.

"I need your help."

I moved in a little closer after shutting the door. "Of course, what's wrong? Did something happen?"

She smiled, but it looked slightly crazed, like she couldn't believe what was about to come out of her own mouth. "Yes. Yes, something happened."

I frowned as I rested my hand on her arm. "Well, what is it?"

Bryn stuck her head around the bathroom door, a wet-looking Ky meowing in her arms and I shrugged my shoulders at her.

"I need you to plan my bachelorette party."

My mouth dropped open and Kat laughed slightly hysterically.

"I'm engaged!"

Continue the Sun City
series in September
2023 with...

STRIP
BARE

ACKNOWLEDGMENTS

Thank you for coming with me on Liv and Bryn's journey, I hope you loved reading about them just as much as I loved writing this book! I can't wait to be back with Liv, Jamie, Bryn and Co in September for Kit and Leo's book: *Strip Bare!* To keep up to date with my releases, don't forget to follow me on social media, Amazon, and sign up to my newsletter. If you haven't already, make sure you go back and read Jamie's story in *Get Even*—**carry on to read the first chapter of *Get Even* for FREE!**

I'm sending so much love to my fabulous ARC team, as well as the wider bookish community for your support. I partnered with some amazing tour companies to promote *Fall Hard,* so thank you to everyone who signed up via Xpresso or RR tours to read the book, as well as the book tour gals and equality book tours.

Big thanks and love to Helena V. Paris, Hannah Kaye, and Rebecca F Kenney for reading an early draft of this book and helping me shape it into what it now is. You guys rock!

Thank you to Erica from Metamorphosis Lit, without whom this book wouldn't be making its way to audio—as well as Tantor for producing it. Thanks also to Jess Amy

Art and Goldenmushroom for creating some gorgeous character art for my books, you nail it every time.

Lastly, thank you to Connor for your unending support and to my own little kitty, Socks, for keeping me company while I write.

ABOUT THE AUTHOR

Jade Church is an avid reader and writer of spicy romance. She loves sweet and swoony love interests who aren't scared to smack your ass and bold female leads. Jade currently lives in the U.K. and spends the majority of her time reading and writing books, as well as binge re-watching *The Vampire Diaries*.

CHAPTER ONE

There were a few things you should probably know. The first was that boys at college were horny. The second was that the girls were horny too. Lastly, I was a firm believer of *Don't get mad, get even*—but I also didn't like to do things in halves. That's how I ended up sandwiched between my ex-boyfriend's brother and best friend.

Brad was moaning in my ear, his breath uncomfortably hot as he pounded away underneath me, wringing small sparks of pleasure from my body. Cody echoed him like this was some kind of pack mating exercise as he moved over me, grunting as he pushed into me shallowly and then harder. The sex wasn't bad. In fact, it was highly satisfying because I knew that Aaron was going to just *die* when he found out about this. Well, maybe next time he promised he loved someone he wouldn't go ahead and fuck their best friend. *Asshole.*

Despite the moral satisfaction, my body was not hugely interested in these guys—mostly because they were idiots and I did generally like to find some sort of intellectual connection in the people I slept with. But... they were pretty, so I focused on the way Cody's golden body flexed in the mirror opposite the bed and the warmth of Brad's hands as they squeezed my breasts. I ran my hands down Brad's abs and gave him a smug smile, there were a lot of them—more than Aaron had for sure. He groaned, tweaking my nipple in one large hand as I sat up and pushed back into Cody's warmth and hardness. His breath stuttered at the change in position and I let out a moan to encourage him on and he began quickly moving again, faster this time. I took the hand Brad still had on my boob and tugged him up so I was sitting in his lap with Cody kneeling behind me, then I directed his hand downwards and pressed his fingers to my clit, giving a loud cry of appreciation. Suddenly they're both scrambling, trying to fuck me harder or faster and I rocked between them with a gasp—*finally*. Whoever said you couldn't have your cake and eat it too was wrong and revenge tasted sweet.

Cody pressed hot little kisses to my neck and heat flooded through me as I reached back and tugged at his blonde curls. I was getting close to the edge as I felt them hit a spot Aaron had never managed to find and suddenly I was shaking through my release, tightening around them until they panted in unison. Brad gripped my waist as they worked themselves to a climax too and Cody slumped against my back as he finished, hair tickling my skin until Brad eased me off them. I was a sweaty mess and I shivered as the cold air rushed over my skin, feeling oddly lonely without them pressed against me. The boys collapsed to the bed on either side of me after ditching their condoms and I smiled at them, kissing one and then the other—now for the *piece de resistance.*

"Say 'fuck me'." I giggled, brushing my dark hair away from my face and holding up my phone to take a very naked photo of the three of us looking thoroughly fucked with our sweaty, flushed skin and smug smiles. Then I found Aaron's contact and hit send, my finger hesitating for only a second over the button.

"Well, this has been fun boys—I'd say call me but, well, don't." My smile was sweet and they looked bewildered as I stood and searched the floor for my clothes —not that they covered much anyway. I'd come prepared to seduce two guys, thinking they might be a little hesitant about betraying Aaron, but really... it had taken surprisingly little effort. My phone vibrated in my hand and my stomach tightened in anticipation of his response. It had been a scant twenty-four hours since I'd got home early and found my boyfriend in my best friend's bedroom—unbeknownst to them. At first I'd gone straight to my room, sat numbly on my bed and waited for my pulse to stop pounding in my ears quite so loudly. Then I'd stood up and walked to the door, ready to burst in there, cause a scene and humiliate them both. But there was something that would hurt them more—*public spectacle.* Plus I wanted Aaron to know exactly how much he meant to his brother. *His* best friend. I'd spoken barely two words to them, just shown up in my skimpy outfit and gave Brad *fuck me* eyes and suggested he bring Cody along for the ride. That was it. They'd sold him out that quickly.

"You're leaving?" Cody asked, pushing out his full bottom lip into a pout that really was cute but dropped it when I nodded my head. I pulled on the lacy black panties I'd been wearing and Brad sat up, concern starting to muddy those big brown eyes.

"Hey, you're not going to mention this to Aaron, are you?"

I smiled. "Oh no, I don't intend on speaking to him again, but you know how he is with secrets."

Brad looked unsure about whether to be worried about his brother and Cody bit his lip. I walked a little closer and brushed a kiss across his mouth. "Wasn't it worth it though?" I asked and Cody melted, a sleepy grin pulling across his face as he decided it was, in fact, worth betraying his best friend for. I supposed I should be flattered.

A knock sounded at the door and the boys both froze like naughty kids with their hands caught in the proverbial cookie jar. I hadn't foreseen a direct confrontation with Aaron at the scene of the crime, considering he'd still been in Taylor's bedroom when I'd left over an hour ago, but this definitely could be fun.

But when I opened the door it wasn't Aaron staring back at me, it was Ryan, their other housemate. His eyes dropped to my still-bare chest and I leaned against the door frame lazily as his gaze found my see-through underwear.

"Do you always open the door in just your panties,

Jamie?" he asked with a small smirk and I looked down at myself as if only just remembering my clothes—or lack thereof.

I giggled like he'd just said the funniest thing I'd ever heard. "Oh, no, I don't make a habit of it. I guess my head still isn't back in the real world yet after spending the last hour with these two." I nodded behind me to where Cody and Brad still lay naked on the bed and Ryan's mouth tightened in disapproval.

"I guess I know why Aaron's on the warpath now," he said, waving his cell phone in our direction, and the boys looked at each other in horror.

"How the fuck did he find out so fast? My dick's barely dry," Brad said and I bit back a grimace at the imagery.

"Something about a picture? I don't know, but if you don't want an awkward scene then you should probably go," he directed the last at me and I batted my long lashes at him innocently while the boys stared at me in something like shock as they realized what I'd done.

"Oh, of course. I'd hate to be an inconvenience to poor, baby Aaron."

Ryan looked like he almost wanted to smile until his gaze dropped to my chest again and he cleared his throat. "You might want to get dressed quickly then."

"Right, yes, it won't take me long. I wasn't wearing much when I got here."

A look of pain crossed his face that only increased as I bent over and stepped into the short black dress crumpled on the floor by the bed and found my shoes. I blew the boys a kiss and they dazedly smiled before frowning, like they weren't quite sure what had just happened and whether they were allowed to have enjoyed it.

"See you later, Ry," I said and he stepped out of the way. He was a complicated one—actually seemed to have a brain rattling around inside his pretty head and a genuine sense of humor. Fuck knows why he chose Aaron, Brad and Cody for housemates. I felt Ryan's gaze on me all the way down the hallway until I walked down the stairs and out of sight.

Sometimes, revenge was a dish best served hot. Sure, I could have walked into Taylor's bedroom, found her and Aaron tangled together and had that image burned into my brain—but I'd chosen a messier path because I wanted them to *hurt*. Aaron would hate my public fuck-you and Taylor was about to get what was coming to her too. She'd clung to me since Freshman year and I could admit that I had clung right back, I'd never had real friends before and I'd thought I'd found that with Taylor and Aaron. But the truth was, Taylor needed me more than I needed her. I'd always been independent, never really had much choice in the matter, but she had always had someone willing to bail her out, to wipe her tears or throw money at her problems. Usually her mom.

At the end of the day, Taylor was a rich white girl and her mom had taught her the most important rule: *never cause a scene.* If she knew half the shit her precious baby girl got up to... I smirked but shook my head as I closed the front door behind me. I didn't want to involve her mom. I wanted Taylor to know what it felt like to be alone, to have the person she trusted kick her in the teeth. Figuratively, of course. I wasn't going to beat her ass, even if she deserved it, because that would make *her* the victim. I was done giving her chances or excuses. Sometimes you had to cut off a limb before the poison could spread any further and that's exactly what Aaron and Taylor felt like, poison in my veins, burning me from the inside out until all I felt was white-hot rage. Their mistake, really. The cheating would have pissed me off, but the *lying* was something I couldn't tolerate. Ever. It hit my trigger button like nothing else, probably thanks to my own, sweet mother, and practically ensured that I wouldn't have been able to stop at payback. I didn't need revenge, I needed to *win*. I smiled as my phone vibrated three more times in my hand, Aaron no doubt losing his mind over the photo and the added insult of being ignored. I didn't give a single fuck. There would be time for tears later. For now, I had to go and confront my best friend.

Lightning Source UK Ltd.
Milton Keynes UK
UKHW010625220223
417437UK00004B/104